"I'm not sure what's going on here, Small Town, but something is," Jared whispered.

Mara didn't answer him. She wasn't exactly sure *how* to answer him.

But she was sure of one thing—something *was* going on between them. Something that seemed outside them both. Bigger than them both. Stronger.

She just had to remind herself that in spite of what she felt, she was likely not to have more than this night with him.

And while she was reasonably sure that wasn't going to be enough for her in the long run, right then, in his arms, with their bodies molded together, it was just about as good as it could get.

D0366916

Dear Reader,

This is a book about someone who has everything—
more than everything—being shocked to discover
that he needs to get a life. Jared Perry is super rich,
super powerful, super sexy, and even though he
can't quite figure out why he's suddenly feeling
antsy, the last thing it would seem to be is that he's
missing anything. And then he meets Mara Pratt.

Mara Pratt is not only a plain and simple hometown
girl, but also she's from the hometown Jared
couldn't wait to get out of and never return to. How
could she possibly be what's lacking in his enviable
life? And yet when he returns to Northbridge,
Montana, in order to meet his long-lost—and
notorious—grandmother, he begins to find life
without Mara would be pretty empty.

But in order to have Mara he must also accept the
place she loves and has no intention of leaving. And
a grandfather he's been at odds with for years.

Welcome home to Northbridge!

Victoria Pade

BACHELOR NO MORE

VICTORIA PADE

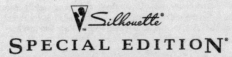

SPECIAL EDITION

Published by Silhouette Books

America's Publisher of Contemporary Romance

SILHOUETTE BOOKS

ISBN-13: 978-0-373-24849-0
ISBN-10:   0-373-24849-0

BACHELOR NO MORE

Copyright © 2007 by Victoria Pade

Visit Silhouette Books at www.eHarlequin.com

Printed in U.S.A.

Books by Victoria Pade

VICTORIA PADE

is a native of Colorado, where she continues to live and work. Her passion—besides writing—is chocolate, which she indulges in frequently and in every form. She loves romance novels and romantic movies—the more lighthearted, the better—but she likes a good, juicy mystery now and then, too.

Chapter One

"Is that someone coming up the stairs? Now? At ten o'clock on a Sunday night? I don't believe these people!"

"I'll take care of it. Go on and do what you were going to do," Mara Pratt advised the elderly woman as Mara stood to give her a hand, pulling her severely overweight body from a recliner.

"Are you sure?"

"Positive. That's one of the reasons I'm here, remember? To run interference for you," Mara reminded.

Celeste Perry managed a tight, weary smile. "I don't know what I would have done without you this last week."

"I don't know what I would have done without you for longer than that," Mara countered.

Celeste gave Mara a warm hug and then pointed at Mara's nose. "You have a little flour smudge from making cookies."

Mara brushed at the spot the older woman had brought to her attention. "Go. Get ready for bed. Tomorrow will be the roughest day yet and you need some rest. As soon as I send this reporter—or whoever it is—on their way, I'll pour you a little brandy and you can wind down."

The rotund woman nodded and disappeared around a corner of the small apartment the Pratt family owned and had rented to Celeste for decades.

Not that they had known they were renting it to the notorious Celeste Perry any more than they'd known her true identity throughout all the years they'd employed her at their dry cleaners. They—like the rest of the people of Northbridge, Montana—had believed they were renting and giving work to a quiet, unassuming woman named Leslie Vance, a stranger new to town in 1970.

The solid, even thuds of steps coming up the outer stairs stopped about the time Mara heard Celeste's bedroom door close. Then a knock sounded.

Wanting to make sure she wasn't too unpresentable if she had to open the door, Mara glanced into a mirror on the wall for a quick check as she called, "Who is it?"

"I'm here to see Celeste Perry," a deep male voice called back.

That was hardly a revelation. As the woman who had—in 1960, after a bank robbery that had rocked the small community—left her two sons and her husband to run off with one of the robbers, Celeste was in high demand.

"That doesn't tell me who *you* are," Mara said, double-checking for any other problems with her appearance.

Earlier in the week she'd been caught off guard by a reporter and photographer at the door and had ended up with an unflattering picture splashed all over town. Not wanting that repeated, she made sure her shoulder-length, cocoa-colored hair was neatly tucked behind her ears and that blush still highlighted her reasonably high cheekbones. She wished that she at least had gloss on lips she thought needed to be a bit fuller, and she noted that, while her straight, thin nose was now unfloured, there was a tiny shadow of mascara beneath one navy blue eye. She ran a fingertip under her lashes to wipe it away and decided that was as good as it was going to get.

"I'd rather not announce my name from out here," the deep voice answered tightly.

Suspicious, Mara moved from the mirror and went to the door. She wasn't about to open it, however, without some information. If the man outside was—like Mara, her siblings and a large portion of the citizens of Northbridge—a supporter of Celeste, it might be okay. But if the visitor was someone who condemned Celeste, or one of the many reporters hounding her for interviews, it could be dicier. So, without knowing who was outside now, Mara wasn't opening that door.

"I don't care whether you want to announce your name. Unless you tell me who you are, you might as well just go away."

"Celes—"

"I'm not Celeste," Mara informed him, cutting off his uncertain use of the name.

"Who are you then?" he demanded, no longer uncertain.

"The question is, who are *you*?" Mara reiterated.

"I'm here to see Celeste Perry," the man repeated firmly, speaking more slowly, as if Mara would understand him better that way. Then, in a louder voice, he added, "If this isn't where I can find her, then where *is* she?"

Mara had faced down any number of muckraking reporters this last week, all of them tenacious, some of them pushy, but none this demanding or insistent. It was almost as if he felt somehow entitled to be. What Mara *wanted* to do was tell this guy to take a hike. The trouble was, if his loud voice roused the suspicions of the state patrolman, on duty to ensure Celeste remained in her apartment under informal house arrest, the officer would come up to the apartment, too. And very little peace would be had tonight.

So Mara knew she was going to have to give a little.

"I'm Mara Pratt," she said. "And no one gets to Celeste without going through me."

"Pratt?" the man echoed. "I know the Pratts. At least I knew them. Cam and Scott—"

"My older brothers. Who I can call and have over here in five minutes to escort you away from that door if you don't tell me who you are."

"I'm Jared Perry."

Oh.

Mara knew who Jared Perry was, even if she didn't actually know him—after all, she'd been only twelve when he'd left town and, at six years his junior, had had no reason to cross paths with him in any memorable way before that.

Still, she was aware that Jared Perry was the black sheep of the Perry family. That he'd left Northbridge the day he'd graduated from high school after a very public argument with his grandfather—the local reverend at the time—at the graduation ceremony. She knew that he hadn't returned since.

She also knew that he had, however, made a fortune as a corporate raider and he was the owner of a daunting reputation. Relentless, ironfisted, unflinching and unyielding—Take-No-Prisoners Perry was how the press referred to him and it had been said by the *New York Times* that if any floundering business, corporation, company or conglomerate caught his eye they might as well just mail him the keys to their headquarters and save themselves some trouble.

He was also one of Celeste's grandchildren.

And someone the older woman would not want left outside on the apartment's small wooden landing in the January cold.

Mara finally unlocked the door and opened it.

And there, in the light of the single bulb, stood a man who looked every inch the rich tycoon accustomed to the awe, respect and probably fear of braver people than Mara.

But still she held her ground and gave him a good once-over to make sure he was who he claimed.

Certainly he was considerably better dressed than any reporter she'd yet seen, wearing a charcoal, midcalf-length cashmere coat that almost—but not quite—camouflaged the impatient switch of his weight from one side to the other. He was tall, imposing and broad-shouldered, staring down at her from a height of at least six feet two inches through eyes that were deep-set, intense and intimidating even from the shadows they were cast in.

Mara mentally matched up what she was seeing with her memory of the pictures of Jared Perry in newspaper and magazine articles in conjunction with some of his business dealings, coming to the conclusion that even though he was far, far better looking in person than in any of his pictures, this was, indeed, the illustrious Jared Perry.

So, without further delay, she said, "Come in," and stepped aside to allow it.

Long, confident strides brought him inside where he seemed to fill the entire room.

Mara closed the door and went around to face him. "I'm sorry for not letting you in right away. You can't imagine how many people have shown up to see Celeste, and not all of them with good intentions. Plus it's late for a drop-in visit."

"I just got into town and I'd like to see my grandmother," he said flatly.

"She's worn out and has a difficult day ahead of her tomorrow—"

"I know. I've spoken with my brother Noah. That's why I'm here now—to do what I can to keep her from talking to the authorities until she has a defense attorney."

"If only you could," Mara said somewhat under her breath. Then, more audibly, "I'll tell her you're here." Only as an afterthought did she add, "Take off your coat and have a seat."

Over her shoulder as she headed for Celeste's bedroom Mara saw Jared Perry remove the exquisite outerwear, exposing a rust-colored sweater that traced the V of an impressive torso to great effect, and dark wool slacks that fitted him so well they had to have been specially tailored for his body.

Nothing shabby about those clothes, either, she thought, pulling her eyes away before he caught her looking.

The apartment's single bedroom was at the end of a short hallway and when Mara reached the closed door she tapped gently.

"Les—" Mara was still having some difficulty remembering to call Celeste by her given name instead of *Leslie*. But that had been the older woman's request so Mara was making every attempt and cut herself short to amend the slip of the tongue. "Celeste," she said through the closed bedroom door, "it wasn't a reporter this time. It's your grandson Jared."

"Jared?" Celeste repeated with the same amount of pleasure she'd shown each time any of her other grandchildren had come by in the past week, the grandchildren she'd only been allowed to view from a distance, until now. "Jared is here?"

"He is. In the living room."

"I'll be right out!" Celeste said excitedly.

Mara turned from the bedroom door but paused for a moment to glance down at her own clothes before rushing back to Jared Perry.

Jeans and a T-shirt—they were hardly going to knock Jared Perry off his feet, but there was nothing Mara could do about it. Although she didn't know why it should matter to her.

Celeste's grandson hadn't taken Mara up on her invitation to be seated. He was still standing, off to one side of the living room now, surveying the space that included a tiny kitchen separated only by a half wall.

"Celeste will just be a minute," Mara informed him when his glance fell expectantly on her.

He nodded, taking a turn at studying her suddenly and unnerving her to no end, especially since his expression gave nothing away and she couldn't tell if he liked what he saw or thought she was the epitome of the small-town yokels he'd left behind.

"Wouldn't you like to sit down?" she asked, hoping to get his eyes off her.

But he neither acknowledged the question nor stopped staring at her. Instead he said, "Mara Pratt."

"That's me."

"I only remember Cam and Scott, but as I recall there were a lot of you."

"Cam, Scott, then Neily, then me, then the triplets—Boone, Taylor and Jon," she said, listing all of her siblings in their birth order.

Jared Perry nodded. "And you're friends with… Celeste?"

Clearly he had his own issues with what to call the woman he—like the rest of the Perrys—only knew vaguely and peripherally as the counter help at the dry cleaners.

"She's worked with us downstairs since she came back to town and realized no one here recognized her anymore because of the weight gain. She was my mom's best friend and since I run the dry cleaners now, we're very close," Mara explained.

"So you're here playing watchdog?"

"Sort of. I'm here to keep her company and look after her and help wherever I can. I couldn't let her go through this alone."

He nodded a second time. "That's nice of you."

"Les—Celeste…your grandmother…has always done a lot for us," Mara demurred, embarrassed by his praise.

The woman in question joined them then, dressed in a pink chenille bathrobe, her coal-black hair released from its ever-present bun to fall to her waist, her ample cheeks rosy with the excitement of seeing another of her grandchildren now that they all knew who she was.

"Jared!" Celeste gushed as she came into the living room.

"Hello," he answered stiltedly, the awkwardness of the moment obvious, just as it had been with other Perrys who had come to visit Celeste in the six days since her true identity had been known.

"I was about to pour Celeste a nightcap," Mara interjected. "Can I get you a little brandy, too?"

"I think so," he said as if it were a welcome suggestion.

Mara left them in the living room and went into the kitchen. She doubted that the cheap brandy she poured from a plastic decanter would be up to Jared Perry's standards, but Celeste lived frugally and it was the only option.

"Let's sit," Celeste said to her grandson, motioning to the sofa as Mara handed them each a glass of brandy.

Celeste lowered her girth into the recliner again and this time Jared Perry took up a spot on the sofa nearby. Where Mara would soon be sleeping just as she had every night for the last week.

"Sit with us, Mara," Celeste invited as Mara was about to retreat to the kitchen again to allow them that slight amount of privacy.

But if Celeste wanted her nearer than that, Mara wouldn't refuse her and perched on an ottoman near the recliner.

Once she had, Celeste's attention centered again on her grandson.

And so did Mara's.

She couldn't help it. Jared Perry was just such a presence in the small space and as Celeste let him know how she'd kept tabs on him and the rest of the Perry family over the years, Mara took more specific stock of what made up the handsome hunk sitting across the room.

His sable-brown hair had a reddish hue where the sun had kissed it. It was cut short on the sides and longer on top, but so meticulously that there was almost an art to the style. His nose was slightly flat across the bridge, with no-nonsense nostrils. His lips were slightly thin, but somehow lush just the same. He had cheekbones that weren't terribly pronounced but sat atop hollows that dipped into a sharp jawline, and a chin with a stubborn firmness to it. There was the shadow of a beard that added to his smoldering good looks but seemed too rugged to go with the sophistication of his attire.

And then there were those eyes—eyes Mara

could now see were so light a blue they were almost colorless. Remarkable, mesmerizing eyes that left her thinking that, if he wanted to, he could make any woman go tongue-tied and entranced with just the right kind of glance.

"Let's get to the reason I'm here tonight instead of waiting to see you at a more civil hour."

Jared Perry's voice—like deep, dark cognac—penetrated Mara's study of him even though he wasn't addressing her.

"I want to talk to you about getting a decent defense attorney," he said to Celeste in an all-business tone that cut to the chase.

"Oh, I don't think that's necessary," Celeste responded with the same not-overly-concerned attitude she'd maintained all through the week.

And with that Mara felt compelled to enter the conversation.

"It *is* necessary," she said, eager for another opportunity to say what she'd been saying from the start. "You should have an attorney who isn't a public defender. You're going to be questioned by the FBI, state police, detectives and the D.A. tomorrow, and your public defender has spent all of ten minutes on the phone with you."

"But that doesn't matter because I didn't do any of what those people will be questioning me about," Celeste insisted, just as she had multiple times.

"Still," her grandson said forcefully, "you don't know what kind of evidence they're going to come at you with or how it might be slanted. With a bank robbery and now the remains of the second robber unearthed to cast suspicions of murder you're in no position to take this in stride."

Obviously Jared Perry was well informed. But Celeste was busy shaking her head at his argument.

"I'm not taking it in stride, Jared. It's just that I didn't do anything," she said again.

"So let the attorney I bring in say that for you," he said, going on to outline all the reasons it was imperative for Celeste to have an accomplished lawyer.

He was eloquent but he didn't pull any punches, and in the process he made Celeste's situation seem very dire regardless of her guilt or innocence. He was so blunt, in fact, that there were a few times when Mara flinched at what he said. Yes, every worst-case scenario was possible if things didn't go Celeste's way, but his harshness stunned Mara and clearly shook Celeste who went from what had seemed to be complacence to all-out, color-drained-from-her-face fear.

He must have seen it, too, because when he'd finished he said, "I'm sorry to take the hard line here, but I've been in touch with the family and when they told me you were sticking with a public defender I couldn't believe it. I knew somebody had to come in here and not sugarcoat things for you. You need a lawyer—a great lawyer—and that's all there is to it."

"He *is* right," Mara put it in a softer tone. "You know I think it's in your best interest, too."

Celeste raised the glass of brandy she'd only been sipping at and threw back what remained of it. Then, for a long moment, she stared blankly at the floor before she said in a weak voice, "I guess I was being naive. If you're both so sure—"

"I'll put in the call right now," her grandson said, whipping out a razor-thin cell phone as if he'd been champing at the bit for the go-ahead.

Seeing that the older woman had wilted in her chair beneath the weight of all her grandson had said to her, Mara reached over and squeezed Celeste's hand.

"It's a good thing to do," Mara assured her, relieved that someone had at last persuaded Celeste, even if she wasn't thrilled with the method. "It can't do any harm for you to have a competent lawyer."

"It can if it makes me look guilty after I've already told the authorities that I don't care about a lawyer because I have nothing to hide," Celeste whispered what had been her contention all along.

Mara hadn't thought Jared Perry was listening but apparently he was, because before she could reassure Celeste he said, "It doesn't make you look guilty. It's no more than they expect of someone in your situation." Then, without missing a beat he began talking into his phone.

"That's true," Mara confirmed before standing and going back to the kitchen, returning with the brandy and refilling Celeste's glass.

The older woman again downed the cheap liquor as if she needed it to steady her nerves.

Then Jared Perry was off the phone and his focus was again on his grandmother—although now that he seemed to have taken over there was no family feeling in the air. Mara had more of a sense that she was witnessing what it was like to have him barge into a board meeting to announce that he had suddenly acquired the company.

"The problem now," he said, "is what I was afraid of when I found out the questioning was tomorrow—I can't get Stephanie here until Wednesday. We're going to have to try to postpone things—"

"Oh, I don't want it put off any longer. I want to get it over with," Celeste said, sounding even more alarmed.

It was alarm Mara understood and she cut Jared Perry off when he seemed on the verge of simply waving away Celeste's anxiousness.

"I know you're sure that just telling your story tomorrow will put an end to everything and you want that to happen," Mara said. "But it's better to be safe than sorry."

Celeste again turned her now-ashen face to her grandson. "Will the authorities let the questioning be postponed? Won't it look like I'm stalling?"

"I don't know if they'll agree. But we'll do all we can, and we don't care if it looks as if you're stalling—"

"*I* care," Celeste said, sounding slightly panicky.

"All you have to care about is getting out of this

and Stephanie is the woman for that. Let her do your worrying. She's the best in her field and she's on the job as of now," he said with what sounded like admiration.

Mara wondered if it was admiration for more than just the attorney's expertise.

"What will this cost?" Celeste asked.

"It won't cost you anything," Jared assured. "I know this woman, she'll be doing it as a favor to me—she owes me one—and whatever expenses come up, I'll cover."

Mara's curiosity about Stephanie and her relationship with Jared Perry increased.

But she concentrated on Celeste, who nodded her acceptance of the financial arrangement but was still more drawn-looking than she'd been since her identity had been revealed and this entire situation had blown up. And Mara was beginning to wonder if she should have turned Jared Perry away at the door after all.

"When will we know if the questioning is postponed?" the older woman asked timidly.

"Not until tomorrow. But as soon as I hear, I'll call you."

Celeste nodded and swallowed so hard it was evident even through her many chins. "I think I need to get to bed now, if that's all right."

"Good idea. We want you on your toes," he decreed.

Mara again helped the older woman out of the recliner. "Are you okay?" she asked Celeste.

Celeste smiled miserably. "Maybe being naive wasn't so bad. I just don't want anyone thinking that I need fancy lawyers and postponements and wheeling and dealing to cover something up."

"No one will think that," Mara assured her. "You have the right to the best defense and that's all this is. Even if it *has* happened fast and…furiously."

Celeste nodded once more but still looked uncertain.

"Go let the brandy do its job and get some rest," Mara urged.

Another nod. Then Celeste turned to her grandson and took his hand in both of hers. "Thank you for coming. And for wanting to help."

"I *am* going to help, you can be sure of that."

It was somehow cold comfort but still Celeste muttered, "Okay…"

Then she said good-night to both Mara and Jared and left them alone again in the living room.

Only when Mara heard Celeste's bedroom door close did she turn to Jared Perry.

"I've been trying to get her to agree to having a lawyer. I just couldn't make myself scare her into it."

One eyebrow arched at her. "Are you saying I shouldn't have?" he challenged.

"I'm just saying I couldn't and maybe just a little lighter touch would have been—"

"I believe in doing what needs to be done— whatever that is, whatever it takes," he said as he put on his coat. "But then I'm usually the person who comes in and gets things turned around when no one else can bring themselves to do it."

Take-No-Prisoners Perry. Mara could see it.

And maybe because of that and because of the change that had overtaken Celeste before she'd gone to bed, Mara wavered a bit in thinking that what he'd just accomplished *was* an altogether good thing.

"It *is* better for Celeste to have a lawyer, isn't it?" she said with a hint of uncertainty of her own now.

"A lawyer who isn't an overworked, underpaid, uninvolved, uninterested public defender? Much."

"This woman you've hired—or enlisted—she'll do everything possible for Celeste?"

He narrowed those ice-blue eyes at her. "Am I hearing suspicion of me again?" he asked, the challenge once more in his tone as he referred to her earlier questions through the door.

"I don't really know you. And you don't really know Celeste. You wouldn't be a wolf in sheep's clothing, coming in here to pressure her into something you have set up to hurt her rather than help her, would you?"

That seemed to amuse him slightly because a small, slow smile made one side of his mouth creep upward. "Now why would I do that?"

"There are people who believe that Celeste was in on the bank robbery and that she killed her lover's partner. There are people who think that at the very least she was an accomplice to it all. And there are other people who think that even if she didn't commit those crimes, there should be consequences for having left her husband and sons the way she did."

"I'm not any of those people."

"But you could want to get back at her for your grandfather's sake or because she abandoned your father or…I don't know, for not being a doting grandmother when you were a kid."

That apparently amused him even more because the other side of his sexy mouth joined the first in an uptilt. "Actually, I've always thought my grandmother and I might be kindred spirits if we ever got to know each other. So no, I don't have anything to get back at her for. I honestly am here to help her."

Mara knew he could just be saying that to cover his tracks if he intended to do damage to Celeste. But she had no way of telling whether he was lying.

And she *had* lobbied for Celeste to have a private attorney. Now that Jared Perry had accomplished that, Mara didn't have much choice but to trust him. And to hope for the best. But that didn't keep her from worrying just the same.

She raised her chin at the man who stood tall, strong and sure before her. "If you're lying and you do anything to hurt her…"

Her threat made him smile full-out—a broad, amused grin that put creases down his cheeks and would have been something to marvel at if Mara hadn't suddenly been so concerned about his intentions.

"What will you do to me?" he asked with barely contained delight

Unfortunately Mara didn't have any threat at all, let alone a good one.

So she merely stood her ground and said, "This had just better be what you're saying it is."

"Careful, I don't think you know who you're dealing with."

"Careful yourself, or you might end up cut off at the knees."

Mara didn't know where that had come from or how she'd managed to make it sound as ominous as she had. She also didn't know what she would possibly do if he pushed it. But still she stared him down—navy blue eyes locked unwaveringly with ice-blue.

Until he blinked.

Not because she'd won the stare-down, but because he couldn't laugh without breaking it.

Then he said, "Relax, Mama Bear, I only came to help your cub." He sauntered to the door, opened it and then added, "I'll be in touch," before he walked out and closed the door behind him.

Mara deflated, realizing that meeting Jared Perry had had its own impact on her as it rippled through her like an aftershock.

An aftershock that brought with it something a little tingly.

Something a little tingly and, surprisingly, somehow exciting.

Chapter Two

Jared Perry was out of bed at 5:00 a.m. Monday morning and on the phone to his assistant in New York by 5:05. That made it 7:05 a.m. New York time so he knew Lloyd was answering at home. It didn't matter. Lloyd was used to Jared calling him at all hours.

After rattling off questions concerning his newest takeover—a sporting-goods business in Colorado—and giving Lloyd instructions for the day, Jared took a shower, shaved, did some paperwork, phoned his man in charge of the revamp of an international electronics firm based in London and watched the clock until the more reasonable hour of 8:30 a.m. That was when he called Stephanie to see what kind of headway she was making with the postponement of Celeste's questioning.

The news was not what he had been hoping for.

Authorities had already delayed the interrogation in order to gather and organize their information, Celeste had a public defender appointed to her so she was represented, and there was no reason for officials to put off her questioning any longer. The fact that Celeste had had a last-minute change of mind regarding representation was Celeste's—and Stephanie's—problem. The stage was set, investigators and the district attorney had made travel arrangements to Northbridge, and they were firm in their determination that today be the day.

"That's it then? It's happening without you?" Jared asked.

"I spoke to the public defender and he'll still be there, only now as my proxy while I participate through a conference call. I'm sorry, J., but that's all I can do on such short notice. I have a death penalty hearing today and tomorrow and I can't leave until it's over."

"I'm worried that if you're not here to coach her, Celeste might say something she shouldn't."

"I'll call her in an hour or so and talk to her, do what coaching needs to be done that way. But all that's really expected of her today is that she tell her story. Of course there will be questions, but to some extent, at this point, investigators and even the D.A. are still on a fact-finding mission."

"It looks like more than that to me when they have a guard posted outside her apartment."

"That's because there's been some concern that she might flee. After all she's managed to keep under the radar for over forty years, which is why there's been talk of arresting her just to hang on to her. But the local cops have successfully kept that from happening and I don't expect that there will be an arrest today either. I think what the feds, the state guys and the D.A. will do is hear out Celeste, take whatever information she gives them back to their own corners, go over it, compare it to the facts and figures and decide where to go from here. If they *do* opt to arrest her it won't be for a day or two and by then I'll be in Montana to handle whatever comes up."

Jared knew that questioning whether or not Stephanie had done her best was unnecessary, so he ended the conversation with a thank-you.

"You know I'd do anything for you, even if you are a hard-ass," the criminal defense attorney responded, teasing him affectionately.

Jared merely chuckled and said he'd see her on Wednesday.

Which left him having to call his grandmother to warn her that the questioning would go on as planned.

He stared at the cell phone in his hand, thinking about placing the call, about who might answer it, wondering if Mara Pratt was staying with Celeste or had only been there the night before as the keeper of the gate until Celeste went to sleep. Would she be back again this early?

If she was staying there or if she'd left and returned already, it was possible she might answer the phone. In fact, it was likely, since she'd announced that no one got to Celeste without going through her first.

And he liked the thought that he might get to talk to Mara Pratt again.

Inexplicable but true.

Not that he objected to speaking to Celeste—he was glad to have discovered his long-lost grandmother, glad for the chance to get to know her, and willing to help her out of the mess he blamed completely on the grandfather he didn't care if he ever saw again.

But what if Mara Pratt picked up the phone rather than Celeste? The possibility gave him a rush and he didn't understand why.

Mara Pratt was what he'd always considered an everyday sort of woman. The kind of woman he connected with Northbridge: wholesome, down-home, salt of the earth. Exactly what he hadn't wanted growing up in the small town.

His fantasies then—fantasies he'd made realities as an adult—had run toward tall, long-legged, sultry, breathtaking blondes. The urbane, well-bred, polished and frequently moneyed women he now encountered in the course of work or play. Women like Stephanie.

And yet, despite the fact that Mara Pratt was nothing at all like Stephanie or like any of his early fantasies and current realities of women, there was something about her that had rung his bell.

Not instantly, he admitted, but Mara Pratt's appeal had definitely sneaked up on him in increments.

He'd been waiting for Celeste, wondering if he'd remember her from his childhood in Northbridge when Mara Pratt had rejoined him in the living room and he'd thought she had incredible eyes. The darkest blue eyes he'd ever seen.

He'd been asking about her brothers when it had occurred to him that her hair was the color of Belgian chocolate, and so shiny and silky he'd had the urge to run his fingers through it.

He'd taken his first—and last—sip of the worst brandy he'd ever tasted just before realizing that Mara Pratt had skin like cream, and a pert nose that was slightly quirky. Then he realized she also had a soft, inviting mouth with an indescribable kindness to it, mingled with a secret sensuality.

He'd been watching her help his extremely large grandmother out of a chair when it had struck him that Mara Pratt had a body that might not be flashy enough to turn every head in the poshest New York restaurant, but there was still a whole lot of allure in her tight, just-round-enough rump, small waist. And her chest had certainly turned *his* head.

No, there wasn't anything at all flashy about Mara Pratt, but she had a free, easy, effortless beauty that was all her own. Serene and understated, it had crept up and apparently taken some sort of hold on him, even more than the extravagant, precision perfection he was currently accustomed to. And understated or not, Mara Pratt packed a wallop that had made it difficult to get her out of his head—all night and here again now.

Which was why he was sitting at the desk in the den of the house he'd grown up in, thinking about her when he had so many other things he should have been paying attention to.

Mara Pratt.

Northbridge, Montana's Mara Pratt.

Cam and Scott Pratt's little sister.

Huh.

Somebody he never would have given a second glance to in the past was suddenly enthralling him. And what made it even more odd was that it was happening at a time when nothing was giving him a charge anymore.

Not a single thing. Not a single person.

Yet the mere idea of talking to Mara Pratt again, of seeing her again, was doing something for him that not even his last multimillion-dollar takeover had accomplished.

And if that wasn't weird, he didn't know what was.

He'd come to Northbridge figuring that besides meeting and helping the grandmother he'd always wondered about, after a little time in the town he'd chafed in, his real life would look a lot better again. He *hadn't* come figuring that anything or anyone here would look good to him.

Maybe he was in worse shape than he'd thought.

Maybe after this he should take a long vacation, he told himself. A couple of months in Europe. Or Tahiti. Or the Bahamas. Or all three. And maybe, when this was all over, that's what he'd do. He'd get away from everything. Lie around somewhere designed for escape. Sleep a lot. Eat and drink to excess. Surround himself with women who would make him wonder what could possibly have made him obsess over some squeaky-clean hometown girl. Blueberry eyes or not.

Good idea, he decided. That's what he'd do. And between a refresher course in what had made him dislike Northbridge and a long vacation, maybe he'd be rejuvenated on the work front, and he wouldn't even be able to conjure up a mental image of Mara Pratt.

Like the one that was lingering in his mind at this moment.

As clear and bright as that skin of hers that he kept imagining the feel of.

Jared closed his eyes and shook his head to rid himself of the unwanted images and equally unwanted—and unwarranted—urges.

Then he opened them, determined to shake more than that, to shake thinking about Mara Pratt and wondering about her and any interest in her whatsoever.

But he still had to make the call to Celeste.

And Mara Pratt could very well answer.

She could very well be there today to support Celeste through the questioning, just the way he intended to be.

Which meant that he'd be seeing her again.

And regardless of how hard he tried—and he *did* try damn hard—he just couldn't make himself hate either of those possibilities.

"Why do you keep looking out that window today, honey? Do you think the Montana version of the Inquisition is going to surprise us and come earlier than they said?"

Celeste startled Mara who had gone to the apartment window while the older woman went to the bedroom to get some hand lotion.

"No, my brother said that since the local cops insisted on having the questioning be as easy on you as possible, the D.A. and the state police and the FBI—and whoever else in on tap—will meet at the police station. Then Cam will bring them here at three," Mara answered, turning her back to the window to face Celeste. "I guess I'm just a little edgy," she added as she leaned against the sill.

"Or is it Jared you're watching for instead of my tribunal? He told you he'd be here before them, didn't he?" Celeste said with a note of intrigue in her voice.

"That was what he told me, yes," Mara said

matter-of-factly. "But no, I wasn't watching for him."

And that was a flat-out lie because watching for Jared Perry was exactly what Mara had been doing. Hating herself for it, but doing it anyway. Several times an hour, every hour since she'd answered the phone, she'd suffered more of that tingling sensation. Simply the sound of his deep voice and learning that he wanted to be here to offer his support to his grandmother during her questioning by authorities had done this to her. He'd told Mara that he would arrive before everyone else, but he'd given no indication how long before, leaving Mara guessing. And checking the alley at every sound to see if it was him.

But apparently even her disclaimer didn't throw Celeste off the scent because as the older woman lowered herself into her chair, she said, "But after you heard he was coming you *did* go and change into those nice gray wool slacks that fit you so well and that baby-blue sweater that I always tell you sets off your eyes."

"I only did that because I thought it was better to present a dignified front to the authorities," Mara said, pulling the reason out of her hat when Celeste was right, she had had Jared Perry in mind when she'd changed clothes.

"Jared is a good catch," Celeste said, ignoring Mara's excuse.

"Nobody says things like *good catch* anymore," Mara said with a laugh. "And I'm not angling to catch any man."

"Maybe you should be."

Mara didn't want to offend the older woman or hurt Celeste's feelings by going into the reasons why—even if she *were* in the market for a man—Jared Perry would not be that man, so she merely said, "I think what I *should* be doing right now is whatever I can to help get you out of trouble so we can both go back to work and do some dry cleaning to make a living."

"Are you trying to tell me you didn't notice how pretty my grandson is?"

"Pretty?"

"Well, he is."

"I'm sure he'd love being called that."

"But you have to admit it's true."

"He's a nice-looking man, yes," Mara conceded. "But he's not my type."

"The two of you would have such beautiful babies together."

Mara laughed. "That's quite a leap."

"And then, instead of just being your favorite employee, you and I could really be family and *I'd* love that!"

"You've thought a lot about this in a very short time."

"There were sparks between you last night," Celeste said.

"Sparks? There weren't any sparks."

"Oh, there were. Small ones, but still sparks. Jared's eyes kept wandering over to you when you weren't looking, like he couldn't resist. Then, when I was opening my bedroom window before I got into bed—you know I like it cracked to sleep—and there he was, standing on the landing after you'd let him out, staring at the door, smiling as big as you please. He wouldn't have been doing that if he hadn't liked you. And you wouldn't have lit up when he called this morning and then changed clothes and gone to that window to look out a hundred times since if you didn't like him, too. Sparks."

"Don't go imagining things," Mara advised.

"I know what I saw."

"Your grandson and I... There probably aren't two less-suited people on the planet."

"I don't see that at all," Celeste said emphatically.

"He's not a small-town boy anymore—if he ever was. He's a man of the world. A jet-setter. A wheeler-dealer. A mover and a shaker."

He was also—by every account in the articles about him and according to talk around town, too—the way Celeste was said to have been in her youth. He was restless and in need of more stimulation, excitement and adventure than could be found in Northbridge. Not to mention that he'd spent his life breaking things apart rather than holding them together, and that was the last thing Mara would let anywhere near her.

But rather than get into things that might give Celeste the impression that she thought one iota less of her than she did, or that she held her youthful actions against her in any way, Mara only finished her argument with, "And I'm nothing but a small-town dry cleaner."

"A beautiful, intelligent, kind-hearted, generous small-town dry cleaner," Celeste amended. "And he'd be lucky to have you."

"He came because of *you*," Mara reminded. "Nothing else has managed to get him back, because he doesn't like it here. Or the kind of people he finds here."

"He doesn't like his grandfather—that's what kept him away. Not hating Northbridge."

Just then the phone rang at the same time as there was a knock on the door, making Mara jump.

"That will be the lawyer calling again, just as she said she would," Celeste said with a nod at the phone, pushing herself to her feet once more. "And I'll bet that's our Jared at the door."

Mara told herself that being startled by the unexpected knock on the door was the reason her heart was beating so fast, that it wasn't because Celeste's grandson had suddenly appeared on the landing outside.

"I'll take the call in the other room. You let Jared in," Celeste said as she headed for the bedroom again.

Reasonably certain that Jared Perry had seen her through the window beside the door, Mara couldn't delay letting him inside in order to compose herself. So she pushed away from the sill and pivoted to the open door, trying to ignore her racing heartbeat.

It wasn't easy when she looked into the now clean-shaven face that seemed even more eye-poppingly handsome than it had in the mental image that had inched its way into her consciousness a hundred or so times since the previous evening.

She was vaguely aware of exchanging greetings with him as she stepped aside to let him in. She devoured the sight of him in that same overcoat he'd had on the night before, open today to show dark-brown wool slacks and a dress shirt to match, worn buttoned all the way to his Adam's apple. There was no denying that he looked spectacular, important and like a force to be reckoned with. All very un-Northbridge-ish.

"Is there a reason you don't want to close the door?"

His voice brought her to her senses and made her realize that she was still standing there, holding the door open.

It also occurred to her that she hadn't taken a breath in that same amount of time.

Taking one now, she shut the door as he removed his coat.

"Is there anywhere I can put this so it's out of the way? I'm guessing this place is going to get pretty crowded."

"I'll take it," Mara said, accepting the soft-as-a-cloud cashmere coat that had probably cost more than her entire wardrobe.

She took it into the hallway and carefully hung it

on a hook on the wall. As she did she caught the faintest whiff of what smelled like fresh, clean citrus. It must have been his cologne, but if she could buy candles with that exact scent she would put them in every room of her house.

"Celeste is on the phone in the bedroom," she said as she rejoined him. "She spoke to the attorney this morning, who said she was going to call back to go over things again just before the questioning got started, so I think that's who Celeste is talking to."

"Stephanie. The attorney's name is Stephanie."

Mara recalled the familiarity in the way he'd talked to the lawyer on the phone the night before and her own initial curiosity about what their relationship might be. Now she thought there was something proprietary in his reference to the woman and her curiosity grew—along with an antipathy toward a person she'd never even met.

"Is she a friend of yours—Stephanie?" Mara heard herself ask before she could stop it.

"Yes, she is."

"A *good* friend?"

Jared Perry was standing behind Celeste's chair and he aimed those mesmerizing eyes at Mara, raising a questioning brow. "Stephanie is a long-time friend," he qualified, still not telling Mara what she wanted to know.

And even though she told herself it was absolutely none of her business, she couldn't seem to keep from pushing it. "A long-time friend who owes you one, which is why she's taking Celeste's case," she said, repeating what he'd told Celeste the previous night.

"Right," he confirmed. Then both of his brows lowered. "Are you worrying again that we're conspiring to do my grandmother harm? Do you think that because we're friends, Stephanie isn't on the up and up? That she'd do my evil bidding or something?"

Mara shrugged in an effort to conceal her relief. Obviously he didn't realize she was trying to get information about the woman and what role she might play in his life.

"Just checking," she said.

"Check all you want. Stephanie is at the top of her field in New York and, as a result of being in demand in a number of high-profile cases across the country, she happens to be licensed to practice law in several states—Montana among them. Were she and I not friends I doubt she'd bother with something like this. But since we are, she took the case. So our friendship is working in Celeste's favor, not against her."

Friends again. But were they more? That was what Mara really wanted to know.

"Is there something about Stephanie's handling of things today that's made you more suspicious?" Jared asked.

"No," Mara had to admit. "She spent a long time on

the phone with Celeste this morning, and afterward Celeste seemed much less nervous about the questioning. We were both happy to learn that there was no reason I shouldn't be able to sit in—and you, too, since it's what you wanted. Apparently, at this point, the attor—Stephanie is insisting Celeste be treated strictly as a potential witness to a long-ago crime—"

"A witness—that's a good way to look at this," he said, sounding impressed with the attorney's point of view.

It served to remind Mara that whether or not he was involved with *Stephanie*, he and the attorney were in a different league, one in which she couldn't compete. He was never likely to be impressed by a small-town dry cleaner. And that was something she had to keep in mind whenever his cologne went to her head.

"I hear cars outside," he said then, pointing his chin in the direction of the apartment's entrance.

Mara returned to the window she'd used all day to watch for Jared. But, unlike the rest of the time, when there had been nothing for her to see, now one of Northbridge's police SUVs was parked below, in front of an unmarked black sedan.

"Looks like the show's about to begin," Mara announced as she watched people—one of them her brother—getting out of the vehicles. "Cam is—"

"I know. He a local cop and will be in on this. I spoke to your brother today when I tried to do what I could to get this postponed," Jared said.

"Well, you're right, he's here with the rest of them."

Celeste must have heard the arrival, too, because she came out of the bedroom carrying the handset of a cordless telephone with her.

"Stephanie wants to speak to you, Jared," the older woman announced in lieu of a greeting.

He accepted the phone and took it into the kitchen to talk.

Mara's gaze trailed along; she was consumed with interest in that conversation. Was it all business or were they saying how much they missed each other? How much they couldn't wait to be together again?

And why should it make the slightest difference to me? she asked herself.

The guy was here today and would be gone forever shortly after this. He was completely inconsequential to her life and so was everything about him. Especially anything he had to do personally or otherwise with Stephanie-the-lawyer.

"Here we go," Celeste said in a hushed voice.

Mara forced her eyes from the man at the other end of the apartment and looked again through the window just as a number of men and women headed for the narrow wooden stairs that led up to the apartment.

Glancing back at Celeste, Mara said, "Are you okay?"

The older woman nodded and settled herself regally in her recliner, feet flat on the floor, head held high, hands resting primly in what there was of her lap.

Jared rejoined them, leaving the phone on the small table beside Celeste's chair. "Stephanie has arranged for the public defender to call her as soon as things get started," he explained just as the sound of voices and footsteps on the stairs made it clear the authorities were drawing nearer.

Mara moved toward the door, but with one hand on the knob, she suddenly couldn't make herself turn it.

She'd been protecting Celeste from reporters and newshounds and gossip seekers all week, but never had the sense that she needed to protect the older woman been as strong as it was at that moment. She felt as though she as about to unleash something that could well be disastrous for someone who had been as important to her, as close to her, as her own mother.

Mara just froze, unable to do what she knew she had to do, even when there was a knock on the door.

"Mara?" Celeste said from behind her.

Still Mara couldn't budge. She just kept thinking, *This could be so awful....*

Without her being aware of his approach, Jared was suddenly there beside her.

She could smell his crisp, bracing cologne. She could feel the heat of his body. The strength of his presence. And when he placed a big hand gently on her arm she absorbed it all like a sponge.

"It'll be okay. There's nothing you can do to keep this from happening," he said quietly, for her ears alone. It was as if he knew exactly what she was going through right then.

Mara managed to look up into his eyes, pale but also warm and kind now.

"It'll be okay," he repeated.

Mara nodded, somehow believing him.

Then he took her hand from the doorknob as if he understood, too, that she couldn't be the one to let in the people who might bring harm to Celeste.

"Go sit with her," he advised. "I'll do this."

Mara swallowed hard. "Thanks," she whispered.

Then, sorry to leave behind the touch of his hand or the strength of his nearness, she did as he'd said and went to sit on the ottoman beside Celeste's chair.

And as Jared did what Mara hadn't been able to bring herself to do—as he opened the door—it occurred to her that regardless of what was or wasn't going on with the Stephanie-the-lawyer, regardless of what Jared Perry's reputation was, she was glad he was there.

Chapter Three

With Celeste's small apartment full of police and FBI, as well as Mara's brother Cam, Mara stayed firmly planted on the ottoman to Celeste's left. Jared stood behind Celeste's recliner, and the public defender sat on Celeste's right, his cell phone on Speaker and positioned so that Celeste's attorney could participate in the proceedings long-distance.

"My lawyer says I should just tell you what happened from the beginning," Celeste said when the video camera was in place to record her statement.

"Go ahead," Cam encouraged.

Mara didn't know if it had been a formal decision for her brother to take the lead with Celeste, but that was what he was doing. It made Mara feel slightly better because she trusted her brother—who she knew thought of Celeste the same way Mara did—to be kind to the older woman.

"I married Armand out of desperation," Celeste began. "My parents had died when I was seventeen, I had no other family, I was working a low-paying retail job that barely afforded me a room at a boarding house, and I had no idea what the future had in store for me. But Armand…" Celeste shook her head as if a hint of awe about the Reverend Armand Perry still existed. "Armand knew exactly who he was, where he was going and what should be done to get there. Armand knew what should be done about everything. He always had all the answers. And I guess that certainty, that stability, was what I wanted at the time."

"This was when? What year?" one of the strangers in the room asked.

"We were married in 1951. Before our first anniversary Carl was born and eleven months after that I had Jack, and there I was—in almost the blink of an eye—a minister's wife with two babies, and I was barely twenty years old. Of course that was how things were done back then—marriage and family, that was the best course for most women. And at first I was grateful to have found that for myself, even if my feelings for Armand weren't of a passionate nature and Armand's feelings for me—well, Armand never let emotion rule."

Something about that caused a small, secret, sad smile.

"Go on," someone ordered.

Celeste took a breath and did as she'd been told. "I found being a clergyman's wife just awful. There were so many expectations of me. From the congregation, from whatever community we were in, from Armand. And then, on top of it all, there were Armand's expectations of me at home—I began to think I would have to be superhuman to live up to it all."

The memory of how daunting it had been made Celeste's eyes widen and her brows arch forlornly.

Mara reached over the arm of the recliner to squeeze the older woman's hand, and for that Celeste gave her an appreciative look before she went on.

"No matter which way I turned, I was just never good enough," Celeste said. "I couldn't meet the demands or reach the high standards imposed on me, from both outside and at home. I loved my boys dearly and I wanted them to love me. I wanted to play with them and make them happy, I didn't want to enforce hundreds of rules and regulations like some kind of tyrant—"

"Which, take it from me, is how the Reverend thinks kids should be raised," Jared contributed.

"I wanted to enjoy my children," Celeste continued after a soft glance upward at her grandson. "But it's Armand's nature to believe that his way is right, and anything different is wrong. And he can be very harsh if his way isn't followed. He convinced me that I was a horrible mother. The worst mother ever. And about the time I was distressed to distraction by his criticisms and the criticism of his congregation, and feeling lower than I'd ever felt in my life, Mickey Rider and Frank Dorian came to town."

Celeste said that fatalistically, covering Mara's hand on hers with her other hand and holding on tightly.

"I went crazy," the older woman said quietly, her tone full of shame. "I didn't even understand myself or what I was doing, but there I was, doing it anyway—slipping out of my marriage bed to meet Frank, drinking at the bar with Frank and Mickey, dancing to jukebox music, kicking up my heels. And falling in love—or at least what seemed like love at the time—with Frank."

Celeste was holding on to Mara's hand so fiercely it was almost painful, but Mara simply endured it, knowing—seeing for herself—how difficult this was for the woman she cared about so much.

Celeste sighed. "Between that…infatuation…for Frank, the desperation I felt at home, and convinced by then that I was a horrible mother and my boys would be better off without me, when Frank asked me to run off with him…" Celeste shrugged as if she'd been helpless against the tides. "I not only wanted to go and be with him, I honestly believed that for the sake of my boys, I *should* remove my bad influence from their lives."

"So you decided to leave with Frank Dorian and Mickey Rider," Cam said.

"Yes. I had no idea Frank and Mickey were

anything but itinerant farmhands, though, or that they were planning to rob the bank. I was shocked to the core when I met Frank at the bridge that night to leave town with him and found out what he and Mickey had done."

There were a few questions to clarify that the bridge Celeste was referring to was the old north bridge that the town had been named after. The same bridge where, during reconstruction, Mickey Rider's duffel bag had been found and near which his remains had also been discovered only recently.

"That night and what followed are important, Celeste," Cam said, bringing her back to the story. "Tell us what happened."

"I'll tell you what didn't happen—Mickey Rider wasn't murdered the way the newspaper keeps saying he might have been. Mickey was mad when I met them at the bridge that night. At first I didn't understand why he cared that Frank was going to take me with him. Then I saw the bank bags and Frank told me about the robbery. I didn't want to go with them after that. But Frank wasn't letting me out of it, and not even Mickey saying I would slow them down changed his mind. Frank said he wanted me with them whether either of us liked it or not. Then Frank and Mickey got into a big fight—like in the movies. There was punching and wrestling and bloody noses and cut faces and fists, and…" Celeste's eyes were wide and tinged with the kind of fear she must have felt that night. "It was awful!"

"Why didn't you run while they were fighting?" one of the female investigators asked.

"It was like my feet were frozen to the ground while my mind raced. I didn't know if I *should* run, if I should go back to Armand, if Frank would come after me, what might happen if he told Armand what had been going on or even—seeing Frank fight with Mickey, I wondered if Frank might hurt Armand or the boys."

Celeste shook her head as if she were reliving her own confusion. "Then, just when it looked like Mickey had the upper hand, Frank seemed to find a last burst of strength. He pushed Mickey off him. Hard. Mickey fell back and hit his head on a sharp rock. There was a shudder—" Celeste shuddered, but it didn't seem like mimicry. It seemed involuntary, in response to the image in her mind, before she ended in barely more than a whisper. "That was how he died."

"Do you need a glass of water?" Mara asked, seeing that Celeste's face had gone gray.

It took the older woman a moment to answer. "No, thank you, honey. I just want to get this all out."

Celeste looked back at Cam as though, if she focused on his familiar face, it would be easier to tell her story. "Frank dragged Mickey's body into the woods to bury him and again I thought about running. But that was when Armand came out from behind the bushes."

Mara's shock was reflected in Jared's expression when she glanced up at his handsome face.

"The Reverend was there?" Jared said.

"Yes. He said he'd followed me to the bridge when I'd left home."

"If he saw that you weren't guilty of anything, why the hell didn't he speak up?" Jared demanded.

But before Celeste could respond to the anger-laced outburst, Cam kept things on a businesslike course. "You told me before that the Reverend recognized you a few years after you'd been living in Northbridge again, but—for the record—you're saying that he was also at the bridge the night of the robbery and was a witness to what you're telling us about that night?"

Celeste nodded. "Yes."

"Did he know you weren't involved in the robbery itself?" Cam asked, again to clarify things for the record.

"Yes. When he came out from the bushes it was to try to get me to go home with him. He said it wasn't too late, that he'd been there to see for himself that I hadn't had anything to do with the robbery. But that if I left with Frank the law would come after me too, the same as if I *had* been in on it, that I would be guilty by association. He even threatened to say I *was* guilty."

"And you still left?" an FBI agent inquired.

"Before I could even think about it, Frank came up from behind us and grabbed Armand. Frank was in a state I'd never seen him in before—enraged and scared and I don't even know what. He said he had to kill Armand and bury him with Mickey."

"But obviously he *didn't* kill the Reverend," a skeptic in the crowd interjected.

"I begged on my knees for him not to," Celeste said. "I told him if he didn't hurt Armand I would go with him, I would do whatever he wanted."

"So you saved his life," Jared said.

"I told Cam that last week. But the more I've thought about it, the more I'm not sure I should take the credit since it was my fault Armand was there in the first place. Because of me, his life was in jeopardy. If Frank had killed him, it would have been my fault, so it was my responsibility to get him out of that situation. But I did tell Frank that if he killed Armand, he would have to kill me, too, because if he didn't, I'd turn him in myself."

Celeste seemed to be tiring, but still she continued.

"It took a lot of begging and pleading and bargaining. I had to swear that I would leave with Frank if only he wouldn't hurt Armand, and Armand had to promise that he wouldn't even say which direction we went when we left. But finally Frank agreed not to harm Armand. He just tied him up in the woods and we took off." Celeste lowered her voice. "And that was when the life I thought I'd wanted out of became something I wished every day that I'd hung on to."

Celeste's head dropped and she shook it back and forth, back and forth, in deep, deep regret.

"Go ahead," Cam encouraged her.

After a moment Celeste said, "When we left Northbridge we went north and, after a few months, ended up in Alaska. By then I was an awful mess. I couldn't sleep, I couldn't stop crying, and when.I'm upset, I eat. A lot."

She laughed a mirthless laugh and motioned to her girth. "I guess you all can see just how upset I was. Frank didn't like it, of course. The pretty, skinny young thing he'd met here had disappeared and I was...I was just a mess," she repeated. "It wasn't as if it was a relationship founded on anything real to begin with, and Frank got more and more disgusted and impatient with me. But still I didn't expect him to steal the little bit of money I'd saved over the years and taken with me when I'd left Armand—"

"The man robbed you, too?" Cam asked, seeming shocked.

"One night while I was asleep," Celeste said. "I don't know why he had to do that. He had all the bank money—of course he'd taken Mickey's share. He kept it in lockers in the bus terminal or train station of whatever city we were in to make sure it was locked away even from me. So it wasn't as if I'd ever touched a penny of it, and my measly $167 couldn't have mattered to him. But yes, he took that, too. And left me alone and penniless in a motel room in Alaska."

Celeste took a deep breath and sighed. "After that there isn't a lot to tell. I didn't really know if the authorities were looking for me or not, but after what

Armand had said I couldn't take any chances. What I wanted more than anything was just to come back here and be with my boys again, and even though I knew that couldn't happen, I started taking any job I could get—usually waiting tables—and every time I'd get enough money saved for a bus ticket, I'd come as far as I could toward Northbridge. I thought that if I couldn't be with Carl and Jack, then maybe I could at least be near them. And that's how I ultimately came home to Northbridge again. But I've already told that story and it probably isn't what anyone wants to hear now."

She *had* told the story—first to Cam when he'd discovered who she was, and later to Mara. She'd told them of living in several towns around Northbridge, hungry for any gossip, any news whatsoever that might give her information about her sons. Then, one day, she'd tested her theory that the weight gain had left her unrecognizable, and she realized it was possible for her to be in the heart of Northbridge without anyone knowing who she really was. So she'd moved back to the small town in order to at least be where she could see her sons—and eventually, her grandchildren—from a distance; she'd lived since 1970 on the sidelines of all but the Pratt family.

"The Reverend has been out of town since you initially talked to me," Cam said then. "And because he's been unreachable, we haven't been able to speak to him—"

"Which will have to be done to see if he confirms your account," one of the state police detectives added. "So if there's anything you'd like to add, this would be the time."

"There's nothing to add. I've told you the simple truth," Celeste said wearily.

From there more detailed questions were asked of Celeste, trying to pinpoint where Frank Dorian might have stashed the bank money before being caught by FBI agents and killed while trying to escape. But Celeste's only answer to nearly every question from then on was that she didn't know. She swore that she'd never seen Frank Dorian again after he'd abandoned her in Alaska, and she had no idea where he went or what he might have done with the money from the bank robbery. And regardless of how many times and in how many variations the questions were asked, she couldn't tell them something she didn't know.

"I only know that I was never the recipient of any of the money Frank and Mickey took," she said, emphasizing each word after some less-than-subtle badgering.

"And, in fact, she was victimized herself by Frank Dorian robbing her of her own money," Jared reminded, his own patience stretched thin.

There were other questions, as well, that Mara saw no purpose for, but Celeste endured each one until the authorities finally agreed, long after dark, that they had no more to ask her. For the time being.

She was warned not to leave Northbridge and assured she would be kept under constant surveillance to make sure she didn't, but on her attorney's insistence, she was released from even informal house arrest and told she was free to leave her apartment.

"We'll be in touch" she was told as they all stood to go, giving the parting an ominous ring.

Mara appreciated that Cam made sure he was the last to follow, spending a moment alone with Celeste, Mara and Jared to tell Celeste that she'd done well, that he hoped the Reverend would cooperate when he returned from his conference and retreat, and that everything would finally be put behind her.

No sooner had Cam left, too, than the telephone rang. It was the call Celeste was expecting from Stephanie to discuss what had gone on. Celeste took the phone to her bedroom, leaving Mara and Jared alone.

"How are you doing?" he asked, sounding as if he genuinely cared.

"I'm glad it's over," Mara confessed.

"Me, too. What's on the agenda for the rest of the evening?"

"Who's thought about anything beyond this?" Mara joked.

"Okay, then," he said, clearly taking control. "Break out that bad brandy and have a shot while I do some shopping. Then I'll fix you both a dinner fit for kings."

"You cook?"

He wiggled his eyebrows mysteriously. "Wait and see."

Jared actually *could* cook. Very well, Mara discovered. He prepared an old-fashioned meal of fried chicken, mashed potatoes, corn bread and salad. It was not fast food, however, and by the time he, Mara and Celeste had eaten, it was nearly ten o'clock.

Celeste was obviously worn out so Mara encouraged the older woman to go to bed. "I'll clean up," she assured, knowing she was taking on a substantial task because while Jared might be a good cook, he was hardly a tidy one.

"I'll stick around and help her," he told Celeste when the older woman seemed hesitant to leave it all to Mara.

That was persuasion enough and Celeste said good-night to them both, heading off to bed while Mara began to tackle the kitchen.

"How do you think she's holding up?" Jared asked the minute they'd heard the bedroom door close behind Celeste, pitching in just as he'd said he would.

"I think she's doing okay, all things considered. We're both just hoping this was the worst of it and that she's cleared from here without being put through any more."

"After hearing what she had to say, it seems to me there *shouldn't* be any more suspicions about her.

But I suppose that's going to depend on the Reverend."

Mara had never heard any one of the Reverend's grandchildren call him by anything but his title so Jared's reference didn't surprise her.

"Cam says your grandfather hasn't been very cooperative," Mara said. "I'm hoping that will change."

"Change is not his long suit," Jared said disparagingly. "Change, forgiveness, understanding, leniency, tolerance, compassion—none of it's in his makeup. At least, not as far as I've ever seen."

"You really don't like him, do you?" Mara asked.

Jared had rolled up his sleeves to cook but now he also unbuttoned his collar button as if he were relaxing more and more the longer they were together. It helped her relax with him, she realized as they worked and talked.

"I don't think it's any secret that my grandfather and I don't get along," Jared admitted in response to her question about his feelings for the Reverend. "Not after that screaming match we had at my graduation—if I know Northbridge, it was well discussed."

"I was only a kid, though," Mara pointed out. "I knew it happened, but I don't remember anything about it. What did you fight over?"

"What it was my duty to do with my life," Jared said as if he were reciting something. "None of the grandchildren had it easy with the Reverend. I knew exactly what Celeste was talking about when she said his expectations of her were superhuman, and I'm sure Noah and our sisters and our cousins would back her up, too. But as the first grandchild and, even worse, the first grand*son*, I don't think I was supposed to be human at all—super or otherwise."

"You had to stay out of trouble," Mara guessed.

"Oh, so much more than that. I couldn't have a hair out of place or a scuff on a shoe. I couldn't raise my voice even in play, let alone say a cuss word. My grades had to be straight As, my behavior exemplary at all times. And as a teenager? Forget about normal teenage rebellion—I couldn't even do what was just plain normal. Like wear jeans—I had to wear dress pants and a dress shirt any time I stepped out of my house because I was representing the Reverend. I couldn't wear jeans in Montana, of all places. Do you have any idea how much I stuck out? And not in a way a teenager *wants* to stick out."

"What about girls and dating?" Mara asked, trying not to think about Stephanie-the-lawyer again.

"Dating? Are you kidding? The Reverend decreed that I should never be alone with a girl, and he made sure I wasn't. My first kiss wasn't until two weeks before the end of my junior year of high school, out behind the church after choir practice. And when I got caught? I can still recall every word of the sins-of-fornication speech he rained down on my head all the way to the religious retreat where I was forced to spend that summer repenting and studying the Bible."

"Just for kissing a girl?"

"It's a wonder it didn't turn me off it for life," he said with an insinuating smile that left Mara thinking much more than she wanted to about Jared Perry and kissing.

Until she forced herself to stop it.

"I do remember all the Perry grandchildren sitting front row center at church services every Sunday," she said then.

"Deathly ill or not, rain or shine, feet flat on the floor, hands clasped in the lap, spines straight, heads forward and eyes cast at our knees," he confirmed, reminding Mara of how Celeste had been sitting in the recliner to face her questioners today.

"But you still haven't told me what you argued with the Reverend about after your graduation," Mara said to prompt him.

"The Reverend had this idea that, as the first grandson, I should follow in his clerical footsteps. I had told him before that I wasn't going to do that, but he'd kept at me. Then, during his speech at the commencement, he actually announced that I was going to study theology. That ticked me off royally, but when I told him again after the ceremony that I absolutely wasn't going to do that and that he had no business telling people I was, he told me that he wouldn't allow my father to pay for my education if I did anything else—"

"He wouldn't *allow* it? Was your father taking orders from him?"

"My father and my uncle have always been under

his thumb. I think the worst thing to come out of Celeste running off was that her sons didn't end up with anyone to temper the Reverend—at least the grandchildren had buffers in our parents and not in living with the old bastard. I love my father and my uncle, but they're afraid of the Reverend, and believe me, neither of them have ever bucked him. So yes, when the Reverend said my father couldn't pay my tuition unless I did what I was told, my father didn't stand up to him. But the Reverend wasn't going to rule me, I made that clear the day of the graduation, and that's when we really tore into it."

Mara was taken aback to think that the Reverend wielded that much power over his sons. "So your parents didn't pay for your college education?"

"Not a dime. That's how I learned to cook—working my way through school. But by then I was where Celeste was when she chose the bank robber over the Reverend—I'd had it with him and everything that went with him. I was willing to do anything necessary to be out from under it all."

The dishes were in the dishwasher and as Mara moved to begin work on the greasy stove she caught a glimpse of Jared from behind as he put leftovers in the refrigerator. For a moment her mind went completely blank as she looked at the best male rear end she'd ever seen.

Then she realized what she was staring at and forced her eyes onto the greasy stovetop as she tried to recall something—*anything*—he'd said that she could use to get back into the conversation.

"You really do identify with Celeste when it comes to the Reverend, don't you?" Mara said, finally. "Last night you said you'd always thought you might be kindred spirits, tonight you've said you know what she was referring to about his expectations of her, and now you're saying you reached the same breaking point she did."

"It's true, I have always thought we might have a lot in common. At least from what I pieced together and imagined about her. The subject of Celeste wasn't allowed in the household so it wasn't as if my father or my uncle, and certainly not the Reverend, ever told me about her. But growing up around here, I heard things, I put two and two together, and I came to the conclusion that she and I might be similar."

"How so?"

"The biggest thing was the fact that she wasn't going to stay here, under the dictatorship of a petty tyrant, when she thought there was more out there for her. And neither was I."

Mara nodded. "I guess that's true. It just worked out a little differently when you left than it did for Celeste."

"Unfortunately."

"So you genuinely *are* on Celeste's side," Mara said then, finally believing him.

Jared had finished putting away the leftovers and

had one hand braced against the countertop near the stove. "That's what I said from the beginning."

"You're so much on her side that it brought you back to Northbridge for the first time in eighteen years—a place you were hell-bent on getting—and staying—away from to put distance between you and the Reverend."

"Right. And I had to meet her. The notorious Celeste Perry? The woman whose name has raised eyebrows in this town for longer than I've been alive? The woman with the reputation the Reverend was determined all other Perrys had to live down? Whom everyone judged us against, deciding whether we might be as no-good as she was?"

Mara flinched at those depictions of the woman she knew didn't deserve to be considered no-good. But she also knew Jared was right—his father and uncle and all of their children had been watched by townsfolk waiting to see if any of them would turn out like the infamous Celeste.

"And even though everything you heard about Celeste was negative—notorious, even—you still embraced being like her?" Mara asked as she surveyed the kitchen to make sure it was clean, and then, once she'd decided it was, leaned against the counter's edge to face Jared.

"Better to embrace being like Celeste than the alternative—I may have been late coming to it, but I *liked* kissing girls. Still do."

The way he said that was too deliciously wicked

not to make Mara laugh—and to think about Jared and kissing again....

There was a clock near where she was standing. Jared seemed to catch sight of it suddenly and realize what time it was. "I should take off," he said, stepping away from the counter.

Mara weathered a surprising rise of disappointment at his words. She was enjoying talking to him and didn't feel ready for it to end.

But short of saying that, she knew she had to let him go, so she merely nodded once more.

"Are you staying here with Celeste or do you just come in during the day and evening?" he asked as they left the kitchen.

"I'm staying with her for now. I hated the thought of her being stressed out and alone. I go home in the mornings—"

"Where is home for you now?"

Was he only making polite conversation or was he interested? She couldn't tell. Probably just making conversation, she decided, remembering Stephanie for an instant.

"Home is the same house where I grew up. All seven of us inherited it and the business when Mom died. My sister Neily and I share the place now, but the boys sort of move in and out when one of them is between other places to live or something," she explained before getting back to what she'd been about to say. "Anyway, I go home mornings, take a shower, change clothes and then come back. My staff at the dry cleaners is keeping on top of things there for me, but I usually check in with them in the afternoons. Otherwise, I'm up here, keeping Celeste company and fielding phone calls and visits from people who show up at the door." Which was far more information than he'd asked for, and to cover that fact she said, "What about you? Where are you staying?"

If he thought that was at all an odd question, he didn't show it as he went into the hallway and retrieved his coat from the hook.

When he returned to the living room with it he draped it over the back of the recliner while he unrolled his shirtsleeves and answered her question.

"I'm staying at my folks' house. As I'm sure you know, they hung onto it when they moved to Billings and use it when they come to town. Nobody's there now so they offered it to me."

Mara was only half listening as she found inordinate interest in watching his big hands unfurl each shirtsleeve in turn, concealing thick wrists, rebuttoning the cuffs with long, adept fingers....

Then he was finished, and she jolted from the study that had set her stomach aflutter for no reason she could fathom.

"Uh-oh, you have a grease stain," she said, noticing it only belatedly and hoping to use it as the excuse for being enthralled by something as mundane as a man unrolling his sleeves.

"Let me treat it before it sets," she said quickly.

"I know Celeste has some of the stain remover we use."

Mara dashed to the kitchen to get the bottle and a clean cloth.

"Handy to fry chicken with a dry cleaner in tow," Jared joked. Adding as she rejoined him, "I guess that towel Celeste tied around me didn't cover everything."

"Hold out your arm," Mara instructed, stepping close enough to do the job. Stepping in to what almost felt like a force field because he exuded such power and strength as he towered above her.

"I've heard you and Celeste mention her working for you," he said as Mara treated the stain. "But shouldn't she be retired by now?"

"She doesn't want to be," Mara answered, trying to ignore what being that near to him did to her. "As she's gotten older she's stopped doing everything but manning the front desk so she just has to sit on the chair there, but she's always said that she'd get bored if she retired. She did admit to me the other day, though, that working at the cleaners has been the way she's kept up with your family—either from one of them coming in, or seeing them pass by on the street outside or chatting with other customers who happen to mention them. She hasn't wanted to cut herself off from that. I don't know if she'll change her mind now or not."

Mara had blotted the stain until it was no more than a damp spot on his sleeve, but somehow she wasn't eager to move away from him. So she gave the now nonexistent stain a few more dabs before she had to quit.

"That should come right out when the shirt is laundered," she told him once she'd forced herself to put more space between them.

"Thanks."

He shrugged into his coat and that also kept her unusually engaged as broad shoulders became the perfect hanger for the garment. Then he went to the door with Mara following behind.

"I talked to my brother when I went for groceries," he was saying along the way, obviously unaware that she was having a problem concentrating again as her eyes attached themselves to the sexy sway of his coat. "The Reverend is due in town on tonight's bus. Noah and I are going over to see him tomorrow, hoping to persuade him the time has come to tell the truth."

"Are you the best person for that job?" Mara asked before she'd considered the wisdom of it.

She was glad when they reached the door and Jared turned to face her with a smile that indicated he hadn't taken offense.

"There are mixed opinions about that," he admitted. "But I want to be there. I've seen all of my family frequently since I left Northbridge—in Billings and various other places—but never with the Reverend around. So I don't know how any of them act with him now that we're all grown up. I'm not sure anyone else will stand up to him if it comes to that. But I'm not afraid to push him if he needs it."

"Just don't push him so much that he denies everything out of spite," Mara said, concern in her voice.

His smile softened. "Don't worry, I've handled negotiations with worse people than the Reverend. I know when to be diplomatic and when to put on the pressure."

Mara didn't doubt it as she looked up into that too-handsome face.

"Anyway," he said then, "I'll let you—and Celeste—know how it goes. And if it seems as though he'll cooperate when he's questioned this time."

"All right," Mara said, more quietly than she'd intended because her mind was wandering again as her gaze focused on his mouth and she recalled his joke about how he liked kissing.

How much did he like it? she wondered.

And was he any good at it?

And was she actually standing here wishing— secretly—that she could find out for herself?

"Okay, then," he said as if he'd been expecting her to say more.

Did he suspect what was going through her mind? Was it written in her expression? Was she all dreamy-eyed or something?

She squared her shoulders and opened the apartment door as if she was ready for him to go. Which she wasn't. But she was afraid something had given away her outrageously inappropriate musings.

"Thanks for cooking tonight," she said perfunctorily.

"Sure," he answered.

But he didn't make a move to leave, and she didn't know why.

"I guess we'll talk to you tomorrow," she added.

That seemed to put him into gear because he finally went outside onto the landing. "Tomorrow," he confirmed as he did.

Then he said good-night, and, after echoing it, Mara closed the door.

But as she locked it she was still thinking about Jared. And kissing. And kissing Jared.

She was also still wishing that he had done it.

But only so she could tell if it had been worth antagonizing his grandfather for, she told herself.

Certainly not for any other reason…

Chapter Four

"Well?"

That was Jared's greeting from his brother when Noah picked him up at nine o'clock on Tuesday morning.

"Well?" Jared repeated, wanting clarification of what his brother was prompting.

"We didn't get a chance to talk when you called last night and before we do this not only do I *want* to know, I think I *need* to know what our wayward grandmother had to say to the police."

Noah pulled his truck out of the driveway of the home in which they'd both grown up, and as they headed for their grandfather's house, Jared related what Celeste had said to the authorities. The part about their grandfather having witnessed the night at the bridge shocked Noah as much as it had Jared.

But it wasn't the only surprise Jared had in store for his brother.

"And the Reverend has known who she is since two years after Celeste moved back to town."

Noah didn't appear surprised at all by that. In fact he looked slightly guilty. "Yeah, I know."

"You know? How?"

"She told Cam Pratt about it. When he and Eden discovered Celeste's identity last week, they went together to confront her. Eden told us after that."

Their cousin Eden had been the forensic artist who had compiled the age-progression that had exposed Celeste.

"And nobody told me?" Jared nearly shouted.

Noah glanced over at Jared and raised an eyebrow at him, shrugging to go along with it. "The Reverend had left town the night before for this conference-retreat thing he's been on, so what Celeste said couldn't be confirmed or denied. We were afraid if we mentioned it, you wouldn't be willing to wait until he got back here, that you might storm the retreat to confront him or something. And we didn't think that was the best way to handle the situation."

"Right, like I'm just a loose cannon," Jared said, none too happy to hear how his siblings and cousins thought of him.

"We know you aren't a loose cannon with anyone else. But we also know how things are between you and the Reverend—you push his buttons, he pushes yours. We just thought it might be like putting a match to a fuse to tell you that he's been aware of who Celeste is for a long time without doing anything about it."

"So you already knew that he recognized Celeste when he went into the dry cleaners one day and she slipped and called him by his first name? That and the way she said it clued him in?"

"Yeah, Eden told us."

"And did you all also know that it wasn't only a matter of him not doing anything to help clear Celeste, that he played on her fears that she could be arrested and charged if anyone else found out who she was? That he used it to punish her, to make her stay away from Dad and Uncle Jack, from all of us, rather than just going with her to the police to verify that she *wasn't* involved in any of it?"

"See? You're angry without hearing his side yet— that's what we didn't want you acting on."

Noah pulled to the curb on South Street and stopped the truck to give Jared a hard stare. "I'm not taking you over there to see him now if you can't get it under control and swear to me that you'll just let him talk. Because if you make this a fight from the start, he'll dig in and nobody'll ever get anything out of him."

"Do you mean to tell me that it doesn't piss you off that Celeste has lived her whole life looking in on us from the outside when all the Reverend had to do was—"

"Yes, it pisses me off," Noah said, a tinge of anger in his own voice to prove it. "A lot of what the Reverend does and always has done pisses me off. But I can keep a lid on it because fighting with him goes nowhere, it just makes him more stubborn. We were all hoping that was something you'd learned by now. But if you haven't—"

"I didn't—and don't—have any intention of fighting with him. But damn it, I thought I was at least being kept in the loop by the rest of you."

"You were. Except for that one thing."

"Go on, put this heap back in gear and let's get there before the cops or this may be a wasted effort," Jared said then, calmly enough to show his brother that he could keep his anger in check.

Noah did as he was told and put the truck back into gear, pulling away from the curb.

"So what'd you think of our grandmother?" he asked then.

"I like her," Jared said unequivocally. "Did you know her better before this, since you live here? Because I didn't have a lot of dry-cleaning needs before I left and I only vaguely recalled her."

"That's what Eden said, too. I knew her a little more than that but not much. Although in the last year or so Mara's done a lot of expansion on the dry cleaners and the construction work has all been mine. That's put me there a lot and since Celeste was there, too…" Noah shrugged again. "She was friendly. Warm. I thought she was just being nice to me because I was underfoot every day, showing an interest to be polite or just to make conversation. But I guess that was her way of getting to know me, trying for some kind of relationship. Seems sort of sad."

Neither of them said anything for a moment.

Then Noah said, "I'm glad she's had the Pratts at least."

"She's definitely close to Mara Pratt," Jared said, feeling the same surge he did each time he so much as thought about Mara, a surge that was a miniature version of what he felt every time he was with her. Like the previous evening, when damn if he hadn't had the ridiculous and misplaced inclination to kiss her....

Noah had turned off South Street and now he pulled up in front of the Reverend's house. It gave Jared an escape from thoughts—and surges—he didn't want to be having about one of Northbridge's hometown girls.

"Did you let him know we were coming?" Jared asked with a nod in the direction of the house.

"I left a message on his voice mail," Noah answered as he turned off the engine and got out.

They walked up to the house together, and Noah rang the doorbell. After waiting for longer than would have been necessary for their grandfather to answer, he rang it again.

"Bad sign?" Jared asked his brother. "Maybe he's not letting me in."

Noah didn't respond, leaving Jared with the impression that it was possible.

It wasn't until the third ring that there was a barely audible call for them to come in.

Noah opened the door, which had apparently been unlocked all along, and went in. Jared brought up the rear, flooded with unpleasant memories as he stepped inside.

"In here," the Reverend said in a weak voice from the living room.

But the man *was* eighteen years older than he'd been the last time Jared had seen or heard him, he reminded himself, so there were bound to be some changes.

The Reverend was sitting in a high-backed wing chair and Jared's first sight of him was slightly shocking. Yes, the Reverend had aged considerably, but Jared hadn't expected him to have withered, too. No longer robust, he was much thinner, white-haired, wrinkled and frail-looking.

He was also not dressed and was still wearing his pajamas and matching plaid bathrobe despite the fact that he had considered it slovenly not to be fully clothed by 7:00 a.m., especially if he was expecting company.

Noah said to the older man, "You don't look well," and it occurred to Jared that what he was seeing was not merely an increase in the Reverend's age, but signs that were alarming even to someone who saw him on a regular basis.

"I woke up a little under the weather," the Reverend answered, gruffly intolerant of the question but with no strength to his voice.

"How are you 'under the weather'?" Noah asked. "Are you just tired or feeling ill or—"

"It's travel. That's all it is. Travel."

Jared didn't think this was the time for tiptoeing around their grandfather the way Noah was. Especially not since the Reverend was suddenly pressing a gnarled hand to his sternum.

"Do you feel weight on your chest? Shortness of breath? Pain in your left arm?" he demanded of the older man.

"Show some manners, you! I'm not even sure you're welcome in my house and you're grilling me!" the Reverend managed to bark.

"Just answer my questions," Jared said calmly.

"Yes," his grandfather gasped suddenly. "And some sickness to the stomach."

"I think he's having a heart attack," Jared said quietly to Noah.

"I'm not having a heart attack! You don't know what you're talking about!" the Reverend wheezed.

Both Jared and Noah ignored the contrary rebuttal.

"It's probably quicker for us to take him to the hospital if we can get him to the truck," Noah said.

"Let's just pick up the chair and use it to carry him out," Jared suggested.

Noah nodded and moved to one side of the wingback.

As Jared passed the sofa he grabbed the crocheted blanket that was folded across the back of it and tucked it around the grumbling Reverend.

"Hang on. We're taking you to the hospital whether you like it or not," he said.

The Reverend cast Jared a venomous look as he and Noah lifted chair and man together.

"Don't expect thanks for this," the older man growled through the pain.

"I wouldn't dream of it," Jared assured him.

It was after eleven on Tuesday night when Mara heard a light tapping on the apartment door. Celeste had gone to bed but Mara was still awake—and worrying—when the knock came.

She hurried to peek out the window. When she saw that it was exactly who she had been hoping it was, she nearly flung open the door.

"Please don't say you're here with more bad news," she said in lieu of hello, keeping her voice soft so as not to wake Celeste.

"I'm not the bearer of the worst news but I don't have the best, either," Jared said equally as quietly, stepping inside.

"Has Celeste gone to bed?" he asked then, glancing around the apartment as he took off his coat and tossed it over one end of the sofa.

Mara closed the door. "I had her take a sleeping pill. I didn't think there was any chance she would rest tonight otherwise."

"We'll try not to disturb her then."

"How is your grandfather?" Mara asked, unable to put it off any longer.

"He's okay. He's in the intensive care unit of the hospital in Billings. We did what I told you we were about to do when I called this afternoon—Noah and I flew with him by helicopter after Reid Walker had him stabilized enough to make the trip."

"You were in too much of a hurry when we talked on the phone to tell me what happened. Did he have a heart attack while you were talking to him about Celeste?"

"No, the attack had started before Noah and I got to the Reverend's house. We found him still in his night clothes, too sick to get out of his chair and answer the door when we rang the bell. He said he wasn't feeling well when he woke up this morning, but he thought it was from traveling."

"He's okay, though," Mara said, confirming what Jared had said a moment before. "And he'll *be* okay?"

"He was still okay when Noah and I left Billings a little while ago. It looks like the heart attack was fairly mild, so the Reverend is expected to recover. On the down side, he's heavily sedated and there are orders that he isn't to be upset for any reason."

"So he can't be questioned by the police," Mara concluded.

"Police, FBI, the district attorney—they're definitely not on the list of visitors allowed into the ICU."

Mara suddenly felt the need to sit down. She got as far as the ottoman and deflated.

Jared had been right—the worst news would have

been that the Reverend hadn't survived his heart attack. But it certainly wasn't the best news that the elderly man wouldn't soon be talking to the authorities or confirming Celeste's account of the past.

"Are *you* okay?" Jared asked.

"I feel bad for saying it when today couldn't have been easy for you, but it was rough here."

Jared sat on the edge of the couch, leaning far enough forward that their knees nearly touched, bracing his forearms on muscular thighs clad in khaki pants to go with his heathered Henley sweater.

"The Reverend's heart attack shook things up around here, too," he said, interpreting what Mara's comment had meant.

"Celeste has been pretty calm since we all found out who she is. I mean, I know her and I can tell that some parts have unnerved her, but she's said that it was a relief to finally have her identity out in the open. But today she was more upset than she's been since this started."

"Concern for the Reverend's health?" Jared asked as if that didn't quite fit.

"She doesn't wish him any harm, but no, it was more that we've both counted on him to back her up. That may have been naive when he didn't do what he should have when he had the chance before, but I honestly thought that now, with everything on the table and so many years gone by, he would just want to put everything to rest himself. And apparently Celeste has thought of him as her ace in the hole, too.

But today… Today we both had to think about what might happen if he isn't around to give corroboration."

Mara's conscience jabbed her, and before Jared had said anything, she added, "I'm sorry. The Reverend is your grandfather and I'm sure his life is more important to you than what he can do for Celeste, and that probably sounds callous—"

"No, actually, it doesn't. I've had the same thoughts today," Jared said. "I know he's my grandfather but, well, if this had been my dad or my uncle it would be different. As it is, I'm sure the Reverend has done good for people—ministering to them and whatever—but when it comes to the two of us, we don't have warm, fuzzy feelings for each other. Today I kept thinking that when he finally *could* do what he should have done years ago, he's just vindictive enough to go and die instead and leave Celeste hanging out to dry once and for all. I know *that* probably sounds callous…."

Mara smiled shamefacedly. "Okay, I won't judge you and you don't judge me, and we'll keep this stuff just between the two of us. Our guilty secret."

"Agreed," Jared said.

"But the Reverend *didn't* die and he should be okay, so everything is just postponed until he has the medical go-ahead to talk to the authorities, right?"

"Hopefully…"

That wasn't very reassuring.

"What do you think will happen if the Reverend

can never verify what Celeste told the authorities?" Mara ventured because it was weighing on her and had been a source of near panic for Celeste, too.

"I talked to Stephanie late this afternoon about that—"

Stephanie. Again. For a while Mara had forgotten about his friendly lawyer. She wasn't giddy over the reminder.

But she still wanted to hear what the other woman had said about Celeste so she forced herself to focus on what he was telling her.

"—having the Reverend admit that he was a witness that night at the bridge and everything happened the way and for the reasons Celeste said, would have made Stephanie's job easier. In fact, she said that if everything had been cleared up today, she wouldn't have had to come to Montana at all. As it is, she'll be in Billings tomorrow morning. She'll talk to the D.A. and see where things stand without the Reverend's input, then come to Northbridge to see Celeste."

Mara sighed. "What a mess."

"No argument there," Jared said.

The ottoman had not been a good choice of seating and Mara realized she was sitting very hunched over. She sat up straight, drew her shoulders back and made a circle with her head to get the kinks out of her neck. She didn't mean it to, but her neck cracked loudly.

Jared laughed. "Wow, you must be tied up in knots."

"We were really hoping that by tonight this would be more or less behind us," Mara said, slightly embarrassed by her popping vertebrae.

"Stand up and stretch," Jared ordered, standing himself.

Mara needed to get off that ottoman so she did as she'd been told. Jared cupped a hand around the ball of each of her shoulders and turned her so that her back was to him. Then his hands moved near enough to her neck so that he could massage her shoulders and press his thumbs into her nape at the same time.

"You *are* tight!" he said.

It hadn't made her any looser to have him touch her so unexpectedly. Or at all, for that matter. Since the first time he'd walked into the apartment his effect on her had been potent and unnerving even *without* physical contact. Having those big hands on her now turned up the volume to loud and impossible to ignore. Her heart was pounding, her blood felt as if it was heating up in her veins and she was hyper-aware of the feel of each of his fingers pressing firmly into her flesh, of his palms cupping her shoulder blades, of the warmth of his skin coming through the angora of her sweater. And what she wanted to do was melt back into his hands, his body, him...

"Take a few deep breaths and try to relax," he said, his deep voice like honeyed whiskey.

Mara took the deep breaths, but what he didn't seem to notice was that there was just no relaxing when someone who stirred something in her that she didn't understand—and didn't want stirred in the first place—was touching her. Besides, the way he pressed into her and then released, pressed and released, again and again, was a whole lot more arousing than relaxing.

"Okay, that's much better," she lied, rolling her shoulders as if they were completely loosened.

Jared got the message and drew what he was doing to a close. And Mara had to remind herself that she'd given the signal to stop and that she had no reason to complain when he did. Although, she *didn't* want him to quit.

Still, she told herself she'd been right to end it and put some distance between them.

"Maybe we should break out that good brandy you brought last night to take the edge off this day, too," she suggested, sounding a bit frantic to her own ears but hoping he didn't pick up on it.

"Okay," Jared conceded.

Was there a hint of disappointment in his tone? Was he as sorry to take his hands off her as she was to have them taken away?

Couldn't be, she told herself. He probably couldn't care less.

"I'll get the brandy," she said, heading for the kitchen as if it offered salvation.

She was back within minutes with two small glasses of the amber liquid, which was of far better quality than Celeste's stock.

As Mara handed one of the glasses to Jared he said, "Noah and I had a long time to talk today."

"Waiting forever in a hospital will do that for you," Mara responded, sipping the brandy.

Neither of them committed fully to sitting again. Jared perched a hip on the arm of the recliner and she sat on the arm of the sofa. But Mara thought it was probably better not to get too comfortable.

"Noah said that when everybody found out who Celeste was there was a lot of curiosity about whether your family would stick by her," Jared continued. "I'd forgotten, but Noah reminded me that your father did the same thing Celeste did—he left his spouse and kids behind, too. Apparently people wondered if it would put you off. Especially you, Noah said."

"Noah had a lot to say," Mara observed.

"That was the extent of it. Our folks and Uncle Jack got to the hospital then and I never found out why everyone was wondering why you—*especially*—might not be too forgiving of something like this."

And he wasn't going to find out now. Rather than address the "especially Mara" part, she opted to address why she *hadn't* held Celeste's actions against her.

"As far as I'm concerned there are a lot of differences between what Celeste did and what my father did. No disrespect intended, but I know *I* couldn't be married to a man like your grandfather and it seems pretty clear why Celeste was driven to commit such a rash act. My father left my mother just because he got tired of life here and of contending with a family. He said he was restless, things here were tedious, and he wanted out, he wanted more fun."

"Not that I held it against her—because I understand the need to get away from the Reverend myself—but it could be argued, based on my grandmother's story of drinking and dancing and having a good time with the bank robbers, that she was restless, found marriage and family tedious and wanted some fun, too."

"I agree that the distinction is small, but what's more important, I think, is that Celeste realized right away that she'd made a mistake, she was sorry for what she'd done—"

"And your father wasn't?"

"We certainly never saw any sort of remorse on his part. We never saw or heard from him again, period. It was as if once he'd moved on, we didn't exist. For Celeste that was absolutely not the case. She's spent her life regretting what she did and doing everything possible just to be near your dad and uncle and her grandchildren."

"Your father leaving your mother would have been forgivable if he'd been more responsible about it and the kids he left her with?"

"I'm not saying my mother deserved to be left— she didn't. She was a great person and his leaving her was an indication of his own lack of wisdom. And I'm not saying that my father leaving wouldn't have hurt the rest of us anyway, but he definitely could have done it more responsibly."

"Like by paying child support? Having visitation?"

"Well, those are just the basics, but sure, that would have begun to show us that he thought as much of us as he thought of himself. But he didn't even do the basics. Your dad and uncle mattered enough to Celeste for her to do everything she could to get back here. She sacrificed any chance of meeting someone else, of starting over again, in order to live here to be near her family. She cared. And knowing her, had there ever been anything your father or your uncle or any one of her grandkids needed of her, she would have stepped up then and there, and risked exposing who she was to help. My father never even knew if we needed his help. While Celeste was watching over you all in the best way she could, making sure everyone was okay, my father was off having his own life, ignoring the fact that he even *had* kids."

"That *is* pretty lousy."

"That's inexcusably selfish and self-centered."

"And it hit you the hardest of all seven kids?" Jared guessed.

Mara was sure he was assuming that was why the townsfolk had been curious about her, especially, supporting Celeste. But what her father had done was not the only reason people would have wondered. She just didn't tell Jared about the other reason.

Instead she said, "It hit us all hard and it is

probably the reason we've stayed so close. It's likely why it's a big deal for us to live in Northbridge and look out for each other."

Jared gave her a small smile. "I'm thinking that the 'especially Mara' part has another reason attached to it that you're skirting around. I'm thinking you probably had something done to you that was like what Celeste and your father did. But you're looking at me, figuring you don't know me, and whatever the 'especially Mara' part is about, it's private and personal and you don't want to go into it because it's none of my business."

Mara merely gave him an enigmatic smile of her own.

"Just answer one question," he said then.

"That depends on what it is."

"Do you have seven kids stashed somewhere?"

That made her laugh. "No, I don't have any kids and I never have had. Anywhere."

He nodded as if he were filing the information away.

He'd finished his brandy and stood to take his glass to the kitchen. "I guess tomorrow will be another big day so I'd better let you get to bed."

Mara followed behind him, stealing a glimpse of a to-die-for rear end until he turned and almost caught her at it.

She left her glass beside his in the sink and then trailed him to the door, fighting a losing battle not to ogle his derriere again, and she was sorry when he slipped on his coat and blocked the view.

"I'll let you know when Stephanie's on her way," he said at the door, turning once more to face Mara.

"And if there's any word on your grandfather—"

"I'll call."

Jared was watching her very closely, peering down into her eyes, holding them with his, when he sort of sighed and laughed a little at the same time, shaking his head, too.

It confused her. "What?" she asked, wondering what had prompted his reaction.

"Why is it that every time I leave here it feels like I should kiss you good-night?"

So it wasn't only happening to her? Or was he picking up on what she'd thought the previous night and what was again going through her head now that they were at the door?

He isn't clairvoyant, she told herself, knowing she had to play this cool or risk giving herself away.

"Have the times we've spent together seemed like dates to you?" she asked as if what he was saying was far-fetched. "Because if this has seemed like dating, you must not have much fun in *your* life."

He smiled slyly. It was so sexy it nearly made her melt. "My life is more about work than fun," he admitted. "But I don't think that's the problem. This seems like it has more to do with you."

Maybe he *was* clairvoyant…

"Well, everyone *does* want to kiss me when they say good-night. There's just something about me, I guess," she joked. "That's how I ended up with those seven kids I have stashed away and don't admit to."

Jared ignored the joke and instead said, "I imagine that every man does want to kiss you when they say goodnight."

His oh-so-pale-blue eyes delved deeper into hers, bathing her in a sensual warmth.

"What would happen if I did it?" he asked in a voice barely above a whisper.

"What would happen?"

"It's been a long time since I've tried to kiss a small-town girl goodnight."

"And then you ended up in Bible boot camp."

"Where would I end up tonight? Slapped for being out of line since we aren't engaged?"

"Things aren't quite that seventeenth-century around here."

"No? Because that's how I remember them."

"Maybe because that was how you were raised. For the rest of us, I don't think things were—or are—different than they are anywhere else. Some people are stuffy and stodgy and narrow-minded, but most of us live in the real world, the twenty-first century. Just like everywhere."

"Really…" he mused as if that opened up new vistas for him.

But were they vistas in which he could see himself kissing her? Because with his clear blue eyes and all of his focus so intently on her, it was an all-consuming notion for Mara.

His achingly handsome face eased into yet another smile, this one even more sinful than the last. Then he began a slow lean forward, toward her.

But the kiss Mara waited for was only a tiny tease of a kiss, a scant touch of his lips to hers before he stood straight again.

"It just seemed like something I should get out of the way so I could stop thinking about it," he said then.

"Well, as long as you've gotten it out of the way…" she repeated, facetiously.

He grinned unashamedly. "That did sound bad, didn't it? All I meant was that I was hoping that doing it would let me stop *thinking* about doing it."

"And did it?"

His grin grew wider. "Guess we'll have to wait and see," he said.

Then, without saying good-night, he left.

It was only after he'd gone that Stephanie-the-lawyer popped into Mara's mind again. Along with the fact that Stephanie-the-lawyer would be arriving in Northbridge the next day.

Was that why Jared had kissed her? In the hopes of getting it out of his system before someone who might be important to him showed up?

That seemed possible, Mara concluded.

And certainly it should have served as a huge warning sign to her.

So why was it that rather than paying attention to that warning, she was wondering if that scant peck of a kiss had cleared his head.

Because it hadn't cleared hers.

Oh, no, instead it had made it impossible to think about anything *except* kissing.

Kissing in a way that would leave her feeling kissed.

And not only had that not-really-a-kiss-at-all kiss made it impossible to think about anything except kissing in a way that would leave her feeling kissed, it had also made her want it so much she could have chased him right out that door to get it.

Chapter Five

"I didn't think I'd see you again today. Did you forget something when you came to change clothes this morning?"

"Nope. I'm here for good," Mara told her sister Neily when Mara let herself into the house where they'd grown up and now lived together.

It was after five o'clock on Wednesday afternoon. Neily was sitting on the sofa in the living room. Mara set the overnight bag she'd been keeping at Celeste's apartment at the foot of the wide staircase in the entryway and joined her sister.

"How come you're home for good? Are you taking me up on my offer to stay with Celeste?" Neily asked. "Because I don't mind. I told you we could trade off."

Mara plopped down on the easy chair facing the couch as Neily closed the book she'd apparently been reading and laid it in her lap.

"Celeste and I talked about it over lunch today and she said she didn't think she needed a babysitter anymore."

"She's ready to have some privacy," Neily guessed.

"I think that's part of it. The apartment is small and she's lived there alone all these years. But also, now that she's told her story, everything is up to the Reverend. His health and the need for him to confirm or deny what she's said have put him at the center of the investigation. Her phone isn't ringing off the hook, no one is coming to the apartment, things have died down for her."

"She doesn't need a buffer anymore."

"Right. She still doesn't feel comfortable going out of the apartment, so we'll have to check in on her, visit with her every day and make sure she has whatever she needs. But she knows I should get back to work, and she said she thought she'd be okay if I did that and went ahead and came home, too."

"So you get to sleep in your own bed again rather than on her couch! But will you be able to or will you worry about her?"

"I think it'll be okay. Celeste has Jared and Stephanie-the-lawyer in on things now, too. They're giving more moral support and big-gun legal advice. That's why I came home now—Jared just brought Stephanie-the-lawyer to talk to Celeste."

"Didn't they want to talk with you there?"

"Oh, sure. I could have stayed. I just didn't want to. It seemed as if Celeste talking with her legal counsel should be confidential, so I left her to it."

"Did Jared Perry leave, too?" Neily asked.

"No, he stayed. But he hired Stephanie-the-lawyer and he's connected to her, and Celeste is his grand-mother, so it made more sense that he be there than me."

Neily frowned comically. "Why do you keep calling her 'Stephanie-the-lawyer' like that?"

"I don't know. That's just how I think of her."

"You also say it kind of negatively. Don't you like her?"

"I just met her half an hour ago," Mara said as if liking the other woman or not liking her was the furthest thing from her mind when, in fact, she hadn't had positive feelings about the attorney even before meeting her. And for absolutely no reason.

"What's she like—Stephanie-the-lawyer?" Neily asked, making a joke out of the title Mara had given her.

"She's every man's dream, every normal woman's nightmare—she's as tall as a model, she has flowing blond hair, she's probably about a 32 D-cup—tiny through the middle but plenty up front. She has a face right out of a makeup ad. She's smart, accomplished, clever. She was dressed in a leather suit with a short, tight skirt that I could never get away with because you have to have that runway height and bearing, and I don't have either. And she's sporting about a three-carat engagement ring."

"You said she's *connected* to Jared Perry—is he who she's engaged to?"

"I think so. He didn't introduce her that way but he did give her a hug and a kiss when she came in."

And even if the kiss hadn't been any steamier than the one he'd given Mara the night before, Mara hadn't gotten a hug. And because she'd assumed Jared was engaged to Stephanie-the-lawyer, Mara had suddenly felt like an outsider. Someone who didn't belong in a group that consisted of grandmother, grandson and grandson's fiancée. And that was the real reason she'd insisted she not be a part of the discussion.

"Well, if Stephanie-the-lawyer is half as hot as you say she is, and she and Jared Perry are together, they must be the world's most beautiful couple because he's…he's *something!*" Neily said, obviously at a loss for an adjective that would do Jared justice.

"You've seen him?"

"I needed to stop for milk and eggs before I came home from work on Monday night. He was coming out of Walt's Liquor just ahead of where I parked on Main and I followed him to the grocery store."

"He cooked dinner for us that night," Mara explained. She and her sister hadn't had much time to catch up before now. "He went out to buy the fixings after Celeste's questioning. And some brandy because he said the kind Celeste had was bad. That must have been when you saw him."

"It seemed as if he was in a hurry so I didn't bother him," Neily said, "but I sure got an eyeful. No one would ever guess he was originally from around here. I mean, talk about the cosmopolitan man! Even Cassie Walker's tennis-shoe tycoon looks more like one of us. Jared is…I don't know, he just has an air about him that shouts *Metropolis*, with a capital *M*. He had on this coat—"

"Oh, I know that coat—"

"It must have cost what we pay in annual taxes on the house. Stephanie-the-lawyer's leather suit couldn't possibly be better than that coat. The wind was sort of whipping it out behind him, and he had the collar turned up, and he had on black leather gloves, and he's tall, and he has those movie-star good looks—" Neily's eyes were as wide as if she'd just seen Jared that minute. "Everyone stopped and stared and I have to say, he was something to stare at."

So it isn't only me, Mara thought. Although she didn't know that she was any happier with the idea that her sister was bowled over by Jared than she was that he was involved with Stephanie-the-lawyer.

She'd never been a jealous person before and she didn't understand why she would be now, but what she was feeling did have all the earmarkings….

"He's hard to overlook, that's for sure," Mara understated in response to her sister's accolades.

"What do you think about him?" Neily asked then.

"I think you're right—he's great-looking."

"No, I mean otherwise? Is he personable? More down-to-earth than he looks? Or is he an arrogant jerk?"

"Are you really this interested in Jared Perry?" Mara hadn't intended to snap at her sister.

Neily's expression showed her surprise. "Everybody in town is interested in Jared Perry," she said. "Does that tick you off for some reason?"

Something was ticking her off, Mara just didn't know what. Or why.

But she *had* snapped at her sister for no reason and now she needed to explain it.

"I just wouldn't want you having a crush on someone I think is engaged," she said, because it was the best she could come up with.

"I don't have a *crush* on him. I haven't even spoken to him. And maybe I'd better *never* speak to him. I wouldn't want you to have to start calling me Neily-the-social-worker."

Mara rolled her eyes at her sister's goad as if Neily were making this into something it wasn't.

But she was glad when Neily just went on.

"Everybody's curious about Jared," her sister said. "He's a hometown boy who's gone out into the world and not only made a splash, but a *huge* splash. And now here he is, *sooo* different than when he left. Different even than his family has made him seem when they've talked about him over the years. He's bigger than life. We're all dying to know what he's like now and you have the inside line because you've been with him at Celeste's."

"I may have been with him, but Celeste and the Reverend and what's going on with that old bank robbery are really the only things we've talked about. I don't have any 'inside line' on Jared." Especially not now, when she wasn't even in the inner circle anymore.

"But you've had contact with him that the rest of us, those who aren't related to him, haven't had. You must have formed some opinions," Neily persisted.

Opinions? What she'd formed were more like observations. For instance, she'd observed that Jared Perry could muddle her thinking and distract her and make her tongue-tied and clumsy. That he could turn her from a reasonably intelligent person into a mushy mass who couldn't think about anything but his well-shaped rear end or his piercing blue eyes or how the mere sound of his voice could make her temperature rise.

There was no way Mara was saying *that* to her sister.

So instead she fell back on Neily's question about what she thought of Jared, and said, "He *is* personable and more down-to-earth than he looks, but not in a hometown-boy kind of way, more in a man-of-the-world-who-can-still-relate-to-the-real-people way. He's nice and pleasant. He has a lot of self-confidence but doesn't seem self-centered. He does walk in and take over—I guess that fits since that's what he does for a living—but he certainly isn't the type to wait for someone else to be lead dog. He's easy to talk to. Good with Celeste. He has a sense of humor. And he cooks very well."

He also kisses people he has no business kissing. Particularly not if he's engaged.

But Mara didn't say that, either.

"It sounds like he's almost as good as he looks," Neily concluded. "Together he and Stephanie-the-lawyer must be the nonsuperhero version of the Dynamic Duo."

"I guess."

"It should help Celeste to have them both in her corner."

"Better the Dynamic Duo than the dry cleaner," Mara muttered.

"Uh-oh, what does that mean? Have you been shoved aside by the hotshot grandson and the legal eagle?"

"No, I wasn't *shoved aside*. I told you, it was my decision to leave just now. I could have stayed."

"Still. You're closer with Celeste than the rest of us, you've bent over backward to help her out this last week, and now here comes the big man, taking over, bringing in his resplendently beautiful and accomplished fiancée…"

And Mara certainly couldn't compete with his resplendently beautiful and accomplished fiancée…

"No," she said to stop her sister's assumptions.

"I'm glad for any help Celeste can get. That's all I meant by better the Dynamic Duo than the dry cleaner—better two people who can do more than keep reporters at bay and field phone calls from investigators and play board games to keep Celeste from stressing too much. Better two people who can actually get something concrete done for her."

"If they can."

"If anyone can, I think it might be Stephanie-the-lawyer," Mara insisted. "She's protecting Celeste's rights and making sure Celeste is treated like a witness rather than a suspect, and she doesn't seem to let anyone get away with anything. Which is good for Celeste and certainly not something I could do for her."

"It's good for you, too, if it means Celeste feels more able to take care of herself again and you get to be home sleeping in your own bed," Neily said as if she thought Mara needed reminding.

"Right," Mara confirmed.

So why was she so ticked off?

Was it jealousy?

Or was it because all the way home she'd wondered if she'd ever see Jared Perry again now that she wasn't staying round the clock with his grandmother, and she was aggravated with herself for it?

Or was it because now Stephanie-the-lawyer had taken over as Celeste's right hand and left Mara with nothing to do that made her feel useful to her old friend?

Or was it because Stephanie-the-lawyer clearly wouldn't have any problems seeing Jared—especially if they were engaged?

Or was it because, if they are engaged, what was he doing kissing me last night?

Maybe it was everything rolled into one.

Mara got up from the chair. "I think I'll go unpack and settle back in," she said with a forced calm when, inside, she was more than ticked off; she was a simmering cauldron of things she couldn't quite pinpoint.

"Want to share a pizza later?" Neily asked, unaware of Mara's inner turmoil.

Mara wrinkled her nose. "Maybe. If I get hungry. Right now I'm not."

"I'll check with you when I'm ready," Neily said, opening her book again as Mara left her alone.

The Dynamic Duo—Neily's term for Jared and Stephanie-the-lawyer echoed in Mara's head as she picked up her overnight bag.

The Dynamic Duo...

She climbed the wide staircase to the second floor. To the bedroom that, with the exception of the six years encompassing her marriage and its aftermath, had been where she'd slept since birth.

There was nothing dynamic about that, she thought. Or about her. Nothing cosmopolitan and nothing dynamic. Jared and Stephanie-the-lawyer were money and power and clout and beauty and great clothes, and she was a small-town dry cleaner.

And that was that, she told herself as she closed her bedroom door behind her.

That was that all the way around, including her little flirtation—or whatever the last few days with Jared Perry could be considered. She needed to get back to work and her routine. She had no idea how long Jared or Stephanie-the-lawyer would be staying in Northbridge, and if she *did* see Jared again it would only be in passing.

There was no reason there should be anything more than that from here on.

And it was better that there wouldn't be, she told herself.

She just didn't know why, when it came to Jared, the thought of not seeing him again or of only seeing him in passing seemed so depressing.

Even if he was probably engaged and every bit as wrong for her as her father had been for her mother, and Derek had been for her.

"I tried to get her to share a pizza with me at dinnertime but she said she wasn't hungry. Maybe you'll have better luck now."

Mara heard her sister's comment as she approached the top of the stairs. It was after ten Wednesday night and they'd both been surprised when the doorbell rang. Since Neily was downstairs, she'd called up to Mara to say she'd answer the door. Then she'd called up to say that Mara had a visitor.

Mara had taken a look out her bedroom window,

spotted Jared's rental car parked outside and the low spirits that had robbed her of her appetite tonight had been washed aside by a flash flood of adrenaline.

Besides the multiple questions that had raced through her mind about why Jared was there, she'd been torn between wanting to spruce herself up and not wanting to leave Neily alone with Jared for any longer than necessary. That second part had won out and all she'd done in the way of revamping her appearance was to run a brush through her hair.

So, as she headed down the stairs, she was in stocking feet, wearing a pair of gray sweatpants with a matching hoodie, and wishing she had put on something cuter to lounge around in tonight. But whatever weird feelings she'd had earlier in regards to Neily's interest in Jared, they had kept her from dawdling upstairs and left her in her sweats.

"Here she is," Neily said when Mara was halfway down the steps.

Neily was in her bathrobe and Mara knew her sister couldn't be happy about it, seeing as it was her first conversation with the illustrious Jared Perry. Mara was fairly certain that was why Neily wasted no time saying, "I'll leave you two to your pizza and head for bed. Early day tomorrow. It was good to talk to you, though, Jared."

"You, too," he answered.

Just as Mara hit the entryway her sister turned toward the stairs. But in what seemed like an afterthought, Neily said over her shoulder, "Nice coat, by the way."

"Thanks," Jared responded as Neily gave Mara a nudge and left them alone.

"Hi," Mara said, her confusion about Jared's visit tingeing her tone.

"I didn't get you out of bed, did I?" he asked.

"No, I was just up in my room. Did the meeting with Celeste last until now?"

"That only took about half an hour. Then I rode to Billings with Stephanie for a quick dinner, checked in on the Reverend, and flew back here."

"Flew?"

"My assistant is the best of his breed—even from New York he found me a pilot and a helicopter for hire in Billings. From now on, one call will get pilot and copter to Northbridge to pick me up and then fly me back again when I'm ready. Much quicker than driving."

"I'm sure."

He was holding a pizza box that had apparently been what Neily had referred to and he raised it an inch as he said, "Dinner with Stephanie is always a lot of lettuce and not much else. I'm starving. I thought maybe we could share this while I fill you in on things."

Mara appreciated that he was making an effort to keep her informed even though she wasn't in the center of things anymore. But she was leery, too. Despite how secretly pleased she was to have his late, impromptu appearance at her door, there was also a part of her that didn't like the thought that he might have played devoted fiancé to Stephanie-the-lawyer, sent her on her way to somewhere else and then come to see Mara as if she were his mistress or something. And it was that aspect that kept her reserved.

"I suppose I can trade a few napkins for a slice of pizza," she said. Then, turning to lead the way out of the entrance, she added, "The kitchen is back here."

"I don't remember realizing as a kid what a great house this is," Jared said as he followed her. "You don't see many places built of natural stone, and with the slate roof and the turret and that wide front porch, it looks like it could stand up through anything. Plus the inside is roomy and homey, too."

"We like it," Mara said.

"Did your family build it?"

"No, it's one of the original houses in North-bridge. My mom had a history that's sort of similar to Celeste's—they both lost their parents when they were in their late teens. But where Celeste was left with nothing and turned to your grandfather, my mother had an inheritance. Nothing monumental, but enough to come here, buy the house and start the dry-cleaning business to support herself."

"So she wasn't too financially devastated by your father leaving her with seven kids?"

"Well, the house was hers, so we had a place to

live. And she had income from the business, so it wasn't as if she was left with nothing. But seven kids is no small group to feed and clothe and provide for. I wouldn't say we were deprived, but we ate a whole lot of macaroni and cheese."

The kitchen was big; country styled; and showed its age in the dated appliances, the black-and-white checkerboard pattern tiles on the backsplashes above the countertops; and in the large oval pedestal table in the center of the room. But still there was a quaintness about it all that Jared mentioned and seemed to like as he set the pizza on the table and removed that coat.

"Soda?" Mara offered, snatching a glance at what he had on underneath the coat and noting that he was still wearing what he'd had on when she'd seen him earlier—dark-brown slacks and a cream-colored sweater. And even though she knew it was ridiculous of her, she was hoping that this meant that he and Stephanie hadn't had a little afternoon delight, inspiring a change of clothes.

"Thanks," he said to her offer of soda.

Mara joined him at the table, bringing with her the drinks, ice-filled glasses, plates, napkins and knives and forks.

"Celeste and I were surprised that you didn't stay to hear what Stephanie had to say this afternoon," Jared said as he opened the pizza box, served Mara a slice and then took one for himself before they both sat at the table.

"It sort of seemed like a family thing, which I didn't think I had a place in," Mara said.

He'd taken a bite of pizza and as he ate it he frowned at her response.

But before he could question it, she said, "How is the Reverend?"

"The same. He's still in intensive care, having some minor arrhythmias—not enough to be of great concern but enough so that they're keeping him sedated and he still can't be talked to about Celeste."

Mara nodded as she finished her own first bite of pizza then said, "Did the meeting this afternoon with Celeste go all right?"

"It looks like Stephanie has everything under control—that's why it didn't take long for her to update us. Basically she just made an appearance with the powers that be today. They didn't show her much of their hand, but she thinks that's because they don't have much to show—"

"She thinks they're bluffing?"

"Not completely. They do have Celeste's statement that she was there the night Mickey Rider died, so should the Reverend have a different story—one that implicates Celeste in some way in Rider's death—they'll have a case with a witness against her, and they told Stephanie that they'll try her."

"That's not good news."

"It didn't come as a shock, though. Celeste wasn't expecting to hear differently than she heard. She knows it's a waiting game for now and that the

Reverend can make or break her, depending on what he says when he's questioned."

So, actually, nothing had changed and Mara wondered why he was there to "fill her in on things" when there wasn't any update.

She was considering asking him about that when he said, "I was a little surprised when Celeste told me she'd encouraged you to move back home. It seemed like a good idea for you to keep her company, particularly now when things are hanging in the balance even more."

"I know, I wasn't expecting her to send me packing until this whole thing is over and done with. But she's been fretting all along about inconveniencing me—I'm sure that's a factor. And maybe she's just reached the point where she needs some time to herself."

"She did say that she knows you need to get back to work, but that you'd promised to go up to the apartment before you open in the mornings, have lunch with her at noon and then check in with her again after the shop closes."

"Right," Mara confirmed. "I tried to talk her into coming back to work herself, to stay busy and to keep her mind off things. But she said she doesn't want to face people until she's cleared."

"Yeah, I tried to get her to leave the apartment, too, and she wouldn't do it. Looks like they didn't need to put a guard on her. She's keeping herself under house arrest."

Jared had finished his second piece of pizza and that seemed to be his last because he set aside his plate as Mara slid hers away, as well.

She left the table and went to a cupboard near the sink, reaching high into it for the box of English bitter-chocolate mints she had hidden there. They were her expensive addiction and she had to special order them on the Internet, so she didn't readily share them. But for no reason she wanted to explore, she was inclined to allow Jared some for dessert.

As he unwrapped the foil wrapping on one he said, "Do you think Celeste is right to stay secluded? Will she be shunned or something when she shows her face again?"

"I don't think so or I wouldn't have tried to get her to come back to the cleaners. Everyone's known her as Leslie Vance forever, and people like her. I'm sure there will be a few who will snub her, but I think they'll be in the minority."

"You think if Celeste is cleared and all this blows over she'll be able to go on living in Northbridge without any problem?"

"I do. Why? Would you take her to live with you and your new wife if she couldn't stay here?"

He stared at her. "My new wife? Do you know something I don't?" he asked, finishing his candy.

"I saw the engagement ring on the lawyer's finger."

"It's hard to miss. But I didn't put it there, if that's what you think."

"You didn't?" Mara asked, knowing she sounded

dim but unable to help herself. In the short time since meeting Celeste's counsel, Mara was so convinced Jared was engaged to her that it was difficult to comprehend that it might not be true. "You're not marrying Stephanie-the-lawyer?"

Jared's smile was slow and amused. "Her name is Stephanie *Wilson* and no, I'm not marrying her."

"But you called her at home on a Sunday night, and you acted as if she'd do anything for you, and you kissed and hugged her when she came in, and—"

"We're friends," he said simply. "And I don't know that I acted as if she'd do anything for me. I did say she owed me one and she did—for introducing her to a friend of mine and ending up engaged to *him*."

Mara was embarrassed to have jumped to conclusions and to have let her own imaginings rule the day. But she was also unreasonably happy to learn that she'd been wrong, although she tried to hold back on that by reminding herself that it shouldn't make the slightest difference to her whether Jared was engaged or not.

"It seemed like there was more between the two of you," she said, to defend herself.

"We did date for about a year."

"You dated—for a whole year—and then introduced her to a friend? Is that how you dump women—find them a replacement?"

"Stephanie dumped me," he said.

"Really?"

"Really. And don't sound so intrigued by that idea."

But Mara *was* intrigued. "How come she dumped you?"

Jared grinned, belying the offended tone of voice he used when he said, "Please, feel free to jump right in and ask me the most personal questions."

Mara grinned back at him. "Okay. How come she dumped you?"

He laughed. But he answered. "She said my heart wasn't in it. And she was right."

"What—or who—was your heart in?"

"The same thing it's always been in, or at least what it's been in until lately—work."

His heart wasn't in his work lately?

Of course Mara could have asked, but that would have taken them off the subject of his love life and she didn't want to let go of that yet.

So she ignored the amendment and said, "Was Stephanie your only serious relationship?"

"I'm not sure you can consider her a serious relationship any more than any other one I've ever been in. My track record on the personal front isn't great."

"You can't make a commitment?" Mara inquired, as if it came as no surprise.

"It's more that the relationships just seem to happen on their own in the background while I'm going full-bore toward business—which is just about always what I'm going full-bore toward. But even though the relationships just start out as a dinner here and there, and then maybe a charity event gets thrown in, or a party or a barbecue, things progress, time passes and somewhere along the way, the women start to want the balance reversed—"

"They want you to pay more attention to them than to work," Mara summarized.

"Right."

"And you don't want to do that."

He merely shrugged his confirmation. "Stephanie has also said that I'm not one to follow through. In work or in relationships. In work, once I've taken over a company, I send in my team, I delegate. All decisions are still mine and I have final say in everything, but I'm not in the trenches, my team is. I'm off to the next project. And since I've never made it to marriage— or even gotten close—I guess Stephanie is right, I'm not much on the follow-through there either."

"So you *delegated* commitment to Stephanie to your friend?" Mara joked.

"Also sort of a pattern if you consider that I've done the same thing with two other women I've dated over the years—one who married my financial advisor and the other just had a baby with my broker. I've heard I'm getting a reputation as a matchmaker. Apparently it's being said that if a woman wants a long-term relationship she should go out with me for a while first because when the time comes to commit, I'll be better than a dating service for fixing her up with someone with whom she'll actually have a future."

He didn't seem disturbed by the reputation he

was gaining or by the number of times it had been true.

"And you're okay with that?" Mara asked.

He shrugged again. "I was my financial advisor's best man, and I'll be best man at Stephanie's wedding, too. And I'm godfather to the broker's baby—I'm not holding any grudges."

"So you wouldn't say your heart was in it with any of the women you were involved with."

"No, I wouldn't. I definitely wouldn't say I was in love with any of them. I'd say I was in like with them—I did like them all. But no, my heart has never been a part of the equation. I'm not so sure being *in love* is in the cards for me."

"Ever? With anyone?"

He shrugged once more. "Hasn't happened so far. And I'm not holding my breath or losing any sleep worrying that it might not."

So he never got in too deep. If that wasn't a warning to heed, Mara didn't know what was.

Jared stood and took both plates and the now-empty glasses to the sink. "I've kept you up long enough, I'll get out of here."

"Let me wrap the rest of your pizza to take with you."

"That's okay, keep it. If I take the leftovers I'll stick them in the fridge at my folks' place, forget about them and they'll rot before somebody else stays there and finds them."

"Are you leaving Northbridge?" Mara asked as

she put the box in her refrigerator. She hated that the thought of him going back to New York already made her feel even worse than she had the entire time she'd believed he was engaged. But there it was.

"Not yet," he answered as he put on his coat. "I'm just saying that *eventually* I'll leave and forget to empty the fridge."

His statement instantly brightened Mara's spirits. And that fact only further confused her.

Jared led the return trip to the front door with Mara following behind, trying not to analyze why she was so relieved to hear he wasn't leaving town for good yet.

"So you're back to work tomorrow," Jared said as they reached the door.

"I am. Will you be with Celeste?"

"I'm driving in to Billings again. The family is having a formal meeting with the Reverend's cardiologist. Up to now he's just spoken to whatever family member is at the hospital when he's there. We haven't all been in the same room with him at once to get the complete picture. There's been some talk about a pacemaker if the arrhythmia doesn't stop and we want a concrete sit-down with the doctor before it comes to that—*if* it comes to that."

"Is Stephanie still in Billings?"

Why had she asked that? She knew where it had come from—it was a remnant of that jealousy she'd been in the grip of—but the moment the words were out, she regretted them.

"Stephanie went back to New York—to her *fiancé*, who is not me. The holdup to her getting to Northbridge this time was a court appearance she had to make. Now she'll keep her schedule free just in case, and I can fly her out again on my private plane in a matter of hours if need be. But for now there's nothing else she can do in Montana."

"And she'd rather be in New York with her fiancé, who isn't you," Mara summed up.

"Right," he confirmed with a smile that made it look as if she were amusing him. Then he said, "I don't know what time tomorrow I'll be back, but I'll let you know what I find out about the Reverend. Will you be here or with Celeste or with your own fiancé, who isn't me, who you just haven't told me about before?"

He was fishing for information about *her* personal life and it gave Mara way, way too much satisfaction to know he was curious.

"I don't have a fiancé who isn't you. Not that you're my fiancé," she added, realizing only after she'd said it that her quip was misleading. But her mind wasn't completely on what they were talking about by then because there they were, at an exit point again, and as had happened every other time they'd been in the process of saying good-night, she was once more thinking about kissing. And how he'd kissed her the night before—barely—to get it off his mind and out of his system, and she couldn't help wondering if it had worked.

"So where do you think you'll be?" he asked.

Where would she be?

She'd lost track of his initial question and had to work at remembering that he'd not only been fishing for information on her romantic attachments—which he hadn't gotten much of—but had also asked where she might be the next day so he could reach her.

"As we said before, I'll check in with Celeste in the morning, at noon and again after I close up. In between I'll be downstairs at the cleaners."

"And tomorrow night?"

"There's a basketball game the local guys play at the high school—I usually go. And then we'll end up at Adz afterward."

"We?"

He was still fishing. She loved it.

And out of pure orneriness, she didn't bite and tell him if she'd be with anyone in particular.

Instead she said, "The team and just about everybody who goes to the game heads for Adz to round out the evening."

Jared knew she was purposely keeping him guessing and his expression showed it in another slow smile while his cool blue eyes settled on hers.

"So, you didn't rush out of Celeste's today because you thought I was engaged to Stephanie, did you?" he asked then.

Mara was reasonably sure he was reminding her that she'd had her own interest in his personal life, but she didn't let it shake her. She graced him with a serene smile of her own and said, "I didn't rush out. If you'll recall, I did the dishes first. And no, that isn't why I left. I left because Celeste and I had already talked about my coming home and I was ready to do that."

He grinned as if he didn't buy it but wasn't going to pursue the subject.

For a long moment neither of them said anything; they merely locked eyes in a playfully challenging stare-down. But in the process, something in the air around them shifted just enough so that Mara knew suddenly that she wasn't the only one thinking about kissing.

"Make it better than last night," she heard herself warn with more brashness than she knew she possessed.

Apparently she'd taken him by surprise, too, because a laugh burst out of him, transforming his handsome face with crinkles at the corners of his eyes and sexy lines down the center of each chiseled cheek.

"I'll do my best," he promised just as she was wondering if he might deny the intention to kiss her at all.

Still cocky, though, he raised only one hand to the side of her face, cupping it to tilt her chin as he leaned in and pressed his mouth to hers.

His lips were parted slightly from the start, just enough to be enticing, to entice hers to part, too. He knew exactly the right amount of pressure, of sway and movement, and before Mara knew it, she floated away on that kiss. She lost all awareness of everything but the warmth and possessiveness of his hand against her skin, of the taste of her favorite mint on his breath, of the smell of his clean-scented cologne. She was wrapped up in the sense of restrained power in his big body towering above her, in that kiss that was so devilishly divine it elevated kissing to a new art form, leaving her—when it ended—feeling as if no kiss she'd ever had before was worthy of comparison.

And the odd thing was, when she opened her eyes to peer up into Jared's monumentally handsome face again, expecting to find him smugly enjoying the fact that he'd knocked her socks off with that kiss, instead she discovered that he appeared to be as stunned by it as she was.

"Huh…" he muttered.

Then, without another word, he opened the door and went out.

And it struck Mara as she watched him go that he'd been right when he'd chosen kissing girls over becoming a clergyman, even at the cost of antagonizing his grandfather.

Because regardless of how good he might have proven to be at delivering a sermon, it couldn't possibly have been better than he was at kissing.

Chapter Six

"I will. You, too. Have a nice rest of the—oof!"

Mara was walking out of Adz, the local restaurant and bar, looking back into the place to call her goodbyes when she found herself face-first in someone's chest, with sturdy arms around her to catch her.

"Oh, excuse me!" she exclaimed before glancing up at the man she'd kept an eye out for all day and evening, the man she'd only in the last few minutes given up hope of seeing. "Jared!"

"Mara," he greeted, taking their collision calmly.

"I'm sorry. I should have been watching where I was going. Did I hurt you?"

"I think I'll survive. What about you?"

"You made a good catch—I'm fine," she said, too thrilled to finally have him there and starting to notice how nice it was to be in his arms. Arms he could have removed but hadn't.

She couldn't just melt into him the way every inch of her wanted to, however, so she drew her shoulders back. But in the middle of the fantasy of him not letting go, holding tight and pulling her in closer, he did what those drawn-back shoulders had told him to do and released her.

Damn.

"Where are you headed?" he asked as they both stepped out onto the sidewalk.

"Home," Mara answered, pulling her coat closed against the frigid January wind. Then, with a nod over her shoulder at the restaurant, she said, "But just about everybody is still inside if you've come to join the party."

"I only came to see you."

No statement that simple should have been able to catapult her into elation. But it did.

"Can I buy you a drink?" he offered then, seeming oblivious to the chill of the wind as he stood there in The Coat with the collar turned up the way Neily had said she'd seen it, leather gloves covering his hands.

"To tell you the truth, I only had tea when I was in there. I have a new hot buttered rum mix at home and I wanted to have a cup of it once I was out of the cold for good and settled in for the night. But if you weren't looking forward to seeing everyone else, you could meet me at my house and I'd buy *you* a drink."

"I told you, I didn't come looking for anyone but you," he said with a small smile she could barely see in the dimness of the tall pole lights that lined Main Street and the shadow of that turned-up collar that bracketed his jawline.

"I'll see you at my house then," she said as if she were taking his acceptance in stride, completely concealing that, inside, she was doing a dance of joy.

Then, continuing the illusion, she merely hurried to her sedan parked at the curb next to his rental car, got in and started the engine.

Okay, so she'd spent the entire day and evening on the lookout for Jared, hoping he'd appear at any moment, and when she'd finally conceded that he wasn't going to seek her out today the way he'd said he would, she'd been so dejected she'd decided to console herself with a good stiff drink. And now that she was headed for home with Jared following behind, she felt as if she had a new lease on life. None of that was what should have been going on over a man she knew was not for her—even less for her after she'd learned what she had about him the previous evening.

But there she was, happy at the thought that he was in the car just behind hers, that she was going to get to spend at least a short time with him after all, and that he'd come out into a Montana icebox of a night to find her and only her.

"He passes women off to his friends because he's less interested in them than in his work. He's not the 'follow-through guy' in either category. He doesn't stick with any one thing. Or person. He doesn't live in Northbridge or even like it here. And you're just asking for trouble if you get anywhere near him," she told herself. "Don't you ever learn?"

Apparently not.

Because not even saying it out loud was enough to keep her from being glad she'd overdressed for a workday and a basketball game in her best-fitting gray wool slacks and the silver mohair turtleneck sweater her brothers had given her one Christmas. Or from being grateful that she'd brushed her hair and refreshed her blush and lip gloss the minute she'd arrived at Adz tonight just in case Jared showed up.

Still, she had at least to keep her foot on the metaphorical brakes when it came to him, she told herself as she drove. Maybe she wasn't slamming down on them and stopping things cold, but she wasn't going full speed ahead, either. And as long as she maintained no more than a slow roll, it was all right. Because with her foot riding the brakes she could still slam down on them if she needed to, before she went too far and got hurt. Again.

But a little hot buttered rum on a freezing winter's night with Jared Perry by her side? How could she resist that?

Obviously she hadn't been able to.

But as long as tonight didn't end up in another kiss like the one the night before, it was innocent enough and it was all okay, she decided.

So, as she pulled into her driveway, she forced herself to adopt a firm determination not to let the night end with another kiss, and as long as she stayed with that she could enjoy her hot buttered rum and Jared's company.

Just keep it at a slow roll, she reminded herself as she turned off the car and got out. *Nothing but a slow roll...*

Jared was right behind her as she went up to the house, and she wasted no time letting them both into the blissful warmth inside.

"It feels like it really is going to get to five below tonight," she observed as she took off her coat and hung it and Jared's on the hall tree in the entry.

He was dressed in navy slacks and a navy-and-tan windowpane-checked sweater; the collar of a tan shirt peeked above the sweater's crew neck. The dark blue made his eyes look even more pale, and Mara's maverick brain leapt to that moment in the entryway the previous night when those eyes had locked with hers. Just before that kiss.

That kiss that shouldn't be repeated.

He's just here for hot buttered rum and an update on his grandfather, and that's all, and you need to remember it, she warned herself firmly.

And she fully intended to stick to it.

Foot on the brakes.

In control.

Please...

"I'd start a fire but we're out of wood," she said, then, to distract herself, led Jared back to the kitchen. "Taylor and Jon are supposed to bring in another cord tomorrow, but that doesn't do us any good tonight."

"The hot buttered rum should take off the chill. What about Neily? Is she here? Do you want to ask her to join us?"

"I'm sure she's asleep by now. She has to be up at 4:00 a.m. tomorrow to leave town for a social-workers' conference. She didn't go to the game tonight so she could pack and get to bed especially early."

"We'll be quiet so we don't wake her, then."

Mara had put the kettle on the stove to heat and was pouring brandy and buttered rum mix into two mugs when she said, "How's your grandfather?"

"Better," Jared answered. "The arrhythmia stopped so there's no more talk of a pacemaker, but his doctor still doesn't want him upset so he's put off questioning again."

"Did you all have your meeting with the cardiologist?"

"Eventually, but that's why I'm so late. The cardiologist had two emergencies today that postponed his meeting with us until late this afternoon. Then the family had dinner together before I could come back here."

Mara nodded. "But the Reverend is doing okay?"

"Barring anything changing through the night,

he should leave intensive care tomorrow and go into a regular room, so we're making progress. It just seems slow in getting to the point where he can be talked to by the authorities."

So once again there hadn't really been anything to tell about his grandfather and yet, rather than merely making a phone call to say that—or skipping it altogether—he'd braved awful temperatures late at night to say it in person.

"Did you see Celeste tonight and tell her?" Mara asked.

"I did," Jared said.

So he'd been out anyway.

Don't make more of this than it is.

"I was with her for a little while. She seemed pretty antsy," Jared added.

"I know. I told her I'd go back and stay with her to keep her company, but she wouldn't hear of it. Then I tried to get her to go with me to the basketball game tonight, but that didn't fly either. It would just be really good if the Reverend could be talked to and would confirm her story so she feels like she can face people again."

Steam began to come out of the kettle's spout and Mara poured the boiling water into the cups. The smell of rum and butter and spices filled the air.

"Kitchen or living room?" she asked when she'd stirred both cups and they were ready for drinking.

"Your choice," Jared said.

The kitchen was brightly lit, warm, smelled good

and seemed safer than sitting with him in the other room, so Mara said, "Let's sit in here. We'll be closer to refills," and took the mugs to the kitchen table where they'd eaten pizza at about that same time the night before.

"Seems fitting," Jared agreed as they each took a chair. "We can pick up where we left off when we were sitting here last night."

"Where did we 'leave off'?" Mara asked. She'd assumed they'd covered all the territory there was to cover about his personal life.

"We left off with it being your turn."

"My turn?"

"There was a lot of waiting around again today and I did some asking about you to find out what you were skirting around last night. I understand you were married?"

"That surprises you?"

"I'm not sure why, but it does. Or maybe it does because you've never given me so much as a hint about it. Is it a secret or something?"

Mara sipped the hot buttered rum and welcomed the warmth it brought with it. "If it had been a secret, would your family have known about it to tell you?"

"They didn't tell me more than that you'd been married—no details—and I couldn't delve into it without raising suspicions about why I'm so interested. And I want details," he said, narrowing his eyes to mock-glare at her over the steam rising from his cup as he took a drink of her cold-weather brew.

"Why *are* you so interested?" she voiced what she was thinking.

He arched an eyebrow at her. "Why were you so interested in Stephanie and my past?"

"I have an inquiring mind?" she said with a barely suppressed smile because she'd been beaten and she knew it.

"Well, that's why I want to know about you—I have an inquiring mind, too."

"Yes, I was married," she conceded before the subject of her wanting to know about his personal life could come up again. "To Derek Jackson. Do you remember him? He was born and raised here, two years younger than you, four older than me—"

"I do remember him. A little. The name, more than anything."

"That's who I married."

"Uh-huh," Jared said before taking another sip of hot rum. "How did you get together?"

"Oh, you know, we just knew each other, he was friends with Cam and came around and was nicer to me than any of my brothers' other friends, and one thing led to another—you know, the whole we-fell-in-love scenario."

"Now that's romantic," Jared said facetiously.

"It's a small town, sometimes that's how things happen. They just do—you start to date someone you've known forever, discover you like them more than you realized, fall in love and get married."

"Still not the stuff novels are made of."

"But that's how it was."

"When did you get married?"

"Right after I graduated from high school. He'd just finished college and gotten a position teaching a few classes that wouldn't interfere with him going on to get his master's degree. I had been working at the dry cleaners and was only planning to go on doing that. We'd been dating about a year—which seemed like forever—so we didn't see any reason to wait even though I was awfully young."

"Is that why it didn't work out—because you'd been so young at the outset?"

Mara laughed humorlessly. "No, it wasn't me who wanted out."

"How long *did* it last?"

Mara sipped her drink. "You really *do* want the details."

"Enough of them to understand why Noah said everybody had wondered if what Celeste did in leaving her family would put off *especially* you."

It was Mara's turn to raise an eyebrow at him. "You haven't forgotten about *that?*"

"No, I haven't."

Was she wrong or had he been doing a lot of thinking about her?

"How long did the marriage last?" he repeated.

"The marriage itself? About four and a half years."

"'The marriage itself'?" he repeated.

"That's how long we were married—four and a

half years. But that wasn't how long I had the responsibilities I'd taken on when I got married."

"The plot thickens," Jared said, taking her cup and his and making them second buttered rums before returning to his chair with them and saying, "Explain."

"Derek's mom had died just after he got out of high school and his dad had been diagnosed with emphysema years before that. After we'd been married about two years, his dad's health had deteriorated to the point where he needed too much help to live alone, so we moved into his house."

"To take care of his father."

"Right. I didn't mind. I liked his dad."

"Did Derek mind?"

"Mmm, sort of. He actually got to minding a lot of things as time went by. Things that he hadn't minded before."

"Like what?"

Jared had made the second drink stronger than the first and Mara was careful only to sip it. "Derek started to mind living here—he said he'd outgrown it. He started to mind that the college was as small as it is and that he worked there when he was convinced he could outshine the best and the brightest at bigger universities. He started to mind that he was married when he was suddenly convinced he was God's gift to women—"

Mara cut herself off before she let the bitterness enter.

"He had an affair?" Jared asked gently.

"No, but he had a few students who thought he was really something and that went to his head. He was sure he *could* have had affairs with them if he'd wanted to, and that seemed to set him on the road to thinking about what else might be out there in terms of women. Ultimately he just decided he could have better than me."

"Did he *say* that?" Jared asked, sounding angry.

"Once. Once was enough," Mara said quietly.

"That was why he wanted out of the marriage?"

"Greener pastures. On just about every front— women, work, life. So he shook off this small town—and me and his dad—and he left."

"'And his *dad'*?" Jared again repeated her words.

"His dad was still alive. Failing, but alive."

"You went on taking care of him?" Jared asked in disbelief.

"Someone needed to do it, I'd *been* doing it and there wasn't anyone else—no family other than Derek. I knew how Don felt about being put in a care facility so until he reached the *very* end—the last week of his life actually, when he needed round-the-clock professional nursing—yes, I went on doing what needed to be done."

"So your dad left your mom with seven kids to raise on her own, and your husband left you with *his* ailing father, who you took care of until he died, and nobody was too sure you were going to want any part of defending a woman who had left someone else holding the bag."

"That's about the gist of it," Mara confirmed before taking a bracing drink of hot buttered rum.

"Now I'm surprised you were so forgiving of Celeste, too."

"I told you before, she had better reasons for leaving. She regretted what she'd done, and has spent her life suffering for it."

"Derek didn't show any regret, even after his father had died?"

"He came back to town for the funeral and to make sure he got every penny he could for his father's house and belongings, and to tell me how right he'd been—that it was a great big beautiful world out there and he was on top of it. And that was the last I ever saw of him."

"He didn't even offer you the family china in payment for taking care of his father and doing what he should have done?"

"Nope."

"I'm surprised I don't remember more about somebody who's that big a jackass."

"He wasn't before—not that I'm defending him, it's just the truth. He seemed like a good guy. We wanted the same things, valued the same things. But somewhere along the way it changed for him. He really just started to see himself as some kind of big deal and he went out to live the life of a big dealer—

the kind of life that couldn't be lived in Northbridge, that's for sure."

"And what was back here—"

"Not his problem. But it wasn't something that would have made him stand out in your mind because it didn't happen until later."

"He doesn't own a business I can squash, does he?"

Mara laughed. "I don't know. But if you ever find out he does, go ahead and squash it," she joked.

"So what was the final tally? Four and a half years of marriage—"

"His dad died about a year and a half after that so the whole thing was about six years."

"And you married right out of high school—at eighteen—that means you were twenty-four when it was all over with. What about since then?"

"Since then? I just sort of haven't wanted to do it again."

"Really?" he asked, putting a lascivious bent to her statement and his response.

"Marriage, relationships, that's the stuff I haven't wanted to do again," she qualified in a chastising tone so she didn't give away the fact that she'd been thinking a lot about doing *it* again since he'd come on the scene.

"You haven't dated or anything?" Jared asked.

"Here and there, but not with much enthusiasm. I've put most of my energy into work. Like you."

"Are you taking over Northbridge?" he teased.

"My corner of it," she boasted.

That made him smile. "I'll bet you are," he said as if it pleased him. "But not if I go on keeping you up late every night," he added, standing and taking both mugs with him to the sink as he'd done the previous night with their dinnerware.

"Are you going back to Billings tomorrow?" Mara asked as they went to the front door.

"No, my assistant is coming here for the day— I have some work that has to be done, papers that have to be signed, all that nose-to-the-grindstone kind of stuff."

Mara waited while he put on his coat, wondering if he might say anything about seeing her the next day or evening. Hoping and wishing he would, even as she told herself it was better if he didn't.

And he didn't.

And that took some of the wind out of her sails.

"I'll let you know when anything changes with the Reverend. Or Celeste will, I'm sure."

Oh. So not only was he not saying anything about seeing her again, he was setting it up so that there wasn't any reason to—not even to tell her there was no news the way he had these last two nights.

Had there been something in what she'd said about Derek and her past that had made Jared shy away? Did he think she'd been telling him she wasn't interested in him when she'd said she hadn't dated? That all her energy went into her work?

It shouldn't have made any difference to her if he

took it that way. In fact, it probably *should* have been her message because she *shouldn't* be interested in him.

And yet here she was, trying hard to find a subtle method of getting across to him that she hadn't meant she didn't want to see him.

Don't do anything stupid, she warned herself.

"Are you okay?" Jared asked as he turned up the collar on his coat and then focused his attention on her once more.

"Okay? Sure," Mara said in a voice that came out slightly squeaky.

"You don't look okay. Should I not have made you talk about your ex? Did it bring up bad mojo or something?"

"Mojo?" she echoed, unable not to smile just a little in spite of how torn she suddenly felt. "No, the marriage and the whole aftermath was six years in, now it's been six years out. I'm over it."

He didn't look convinced. "I'm sorry if I made you feel bad."

"It's all right, really. You didn't." At least not by asking about her past. The present, though, that was something else….

"How can I make it up to you?" he asked.

"There's nothing to make up for," Mara insisted.

But still he gave no indication that he was buying that. Instead he was standing several feet away, looking as if he regretted what he'd done.

Then he said, "I know a lot of guys who are

great—hey, I've fixed up a few with great women," he joked.

Mara forced a smile, wondering if this was going to end with him offering to fix *her* up with someone else.

"I also know some guys who have whole other agendas when it comes to women," he continued. "I know one who's all about how the woman on his arm makes him look—it doesn't matter if she's a dimwit or a bigot or a generally rotten person. If she turns heads, he wants to be who she's with. I know another guy who honestly is a gold digger—he has expensive tastes, likes expensive toys and entertainments and doesn't want to work. For him it's all about a woman's bank account, never about the woman herself. Your ex sounds like someone who falls in the same category those guys do. And it probably doesn't make it any better, but I'm betting him leaving was all about him, not about you. It's just too bad he had to cut you down and hurt you to do it. But from what I've seen in my matchmaking—"

Is this where he offers that service?

"—what attracts people, what makes relationships and keeps couples together, is more indefinable and not on the surface. Take Stephanie, for example— she's not hard on the eyes, she's successful, smart and if you'd stayed around for a few minutes the other day and talked to her, you'd know she's a genuinely nice person, too. She's someone any—

every—man *should* want. Yet when I was with her, it was out of sight, out of mind for me."

Jared took a step nearer and his legs were long enough for that single step to close the gap and put him directly in front of Mara.

"But you," he said then, his voice softer, as if he were confiding something. "I can't get you out of my mind at all."

Had she heard that right?

"You can't?"

He shook his head slowly. "And since last night it's only gotten worse."

She really couldn't help smiling, although he'd said that as if it wasn't altogether a good thing.

"Should I apologize?" she asked.

He cracked a smile then, too. "Maybe," he said.

She didn't, though. She just gazed up into his eyes and knew she was already in a world of trouble with this man.

This man who reached a big hand to each of her shoulders in a way that began as if he were offering moral support but almost instantly became a far more sensual massage.

And then he was kissing her again. Softly at first. A kiss that had some contrition to it. Some consoling elements just as his hands on her shoulders had seemed at the start.

But like his hands on her shoulders, his kiss rapidly heated up and before she knew it, his mouth was covering hers, his lips were parted and she was kissing him back for all she was worth.

He wrapped his arms around her then, pulling her in close, holding her.

Her arms seemed to float around him, too, and she laid her hands against that straight, strong back encased in that cashmere miracle Mara wished would disappear. His lips parted—wider than they'd been on Wednesday night—and hers answered in kind, so that when his tongue made its maiden journey her tongue could meet it tip to tip. Welcome it. Maybe even lure it a little until it was making its presence known fully and formidably in swirls and turns and thrusts that deepened the kiss with every second that passed.

Her head was pressed into a cradling hand by then and her fingers were embedded in cashmere and muscle, holding him as firmly as he was holding her. Mara was swept away by that kiss, left unaware of how much time went by, of where they were, of any thought beyond that moment and that kiss and that man and how it felt to have him so near, to be against him, to have his breath and hers mingling, his tongue and hers pairing so peerlessly….

Until Jared began to draw it all to a slow close. His tongue seemed to pull away, reluctantly leaving a more simple kiss that lasted only a few moments before it ended.

And then began again.

And ended again.

Then he took his arms from around her and stepped back, only opening his eyes after he had.

"I don't think that's going to help get you off my mind," he said in a low, raspy voice.

Then he opened the door and disappeared out into the cold again before Mara had regained the wherewithal to speak.

And suddenly she was standing alone in her entryway, staring at her closed front door, her body still warm from being against his, her lips still moist from his kiss.

That shouldn't have happened again, she told herself, recalling her decision on the drive from Adz to keep things between Jared and herself to a controlled roll so that the night didn't end with a kiss like last night's.

It hadn't, though, she thought.

Not technically at any rate.

Tonight had ended with a kiss that was even more derailing.

Derailing and enlightening because it told her just how susceptible she was to Jared.

Yet, despite knowing how susceptible she was to him and that there was danger in that, Mara still went upstairs feeling as if she were beaming from the inside out.

And knowing, too, that if she had the chance to do that kiss all over again, she would.

Chapter Seven

It was nearly ten o'clock Friday night when Jared left his grandmother's apartment. Pausing once he was outside on the landing, he took a few deep breaths. The cold was a relief after the heat of the elderly woman's apartment, and it surprised him how much he relished the clear crispness of the Montana air. It hadn't been something he'd thought he missed. But maybe he'd been wrong.

He and his assistant had put in a long day and when Lloyd had left town around eight, Jared had gone to visit Celeste. He'd wanted at least to check on her and do what he could to break up the empty hours she spent alone in that apartment.

He'd also been harboring the unwanted hope that he might run into Mara.

It was a contradiction to the course he'd set for today. Today was supposed to be a Mara-free day. That was the main reason he'd had Lloyd come into Northbridge to bring him work. Work usually did the trick when he needed a distraction.

But not this time. In fact, the opposite had happened—thoughts of Mara had kept him from concentrating on work and by the time he'd headed for Celeste's apartment he was hoping for a way out of his Mara-free day.

He hadn't gotten it, though, because Mara hadn't been there. She had been earlier, Celeste had said. Several times. But Celeste didn't expect her again until Saturday. And as much as it surprised him to realize he was enjoying something about Montana, as he stood on that landing outside the apartment, it surprised him even more to find himself feeling cheated because he hadn't found Mara inside.

Fate was giving him a hand in keeping his resolve to go one full day without seeing her, he told himself. But it had been fate that had brought him to this town again in the first place. Fate had set Mara in front of him and flipped on some switch that had him nearly obsessed with the small-town girl. After all that, why should fate cooperate now, when he'd decided he should try keeping his distance from her to get his head on straight again?

Fickle damn fate…

After one last deep breath and a resigned sigh to blow it out, he headed down the stairs.

But as he stepped onto the cobblestones of the alley below, a light in the lower portion of the building drew his attention. A light in the dry cleaners.

Celeste had mentioned that Mara had intended to work late, but *this* late?

Maybe it was a cleaning crew or something, he thought as he made his way toward the window.

But he didn't merely leave it at that and pass by. When he reached the window he stopped and nearly pressed his nose to the glass to look inside.

What he saw was the rear section of the dry cleaners—machinery, piles of clothing, clothes draped in plastic bags hanging from a motorized rack, tables and various other things he assumed had to do with the business.

What he didn't see was Mara. Or a cleaning crew.

There was, however, a light on in a room he could partially see into, a room with filing cabinets against one wall, so he thought it must be an office. Mara's office. Where Mara might be.

So he stayed where he was, in the cold, spying like a Peeping Tom.

No one who knew him would have believed it.

But a moment later, when Mara opened one of the file drawers, he didn't care about anything but that she was there. He was seeing her after all.

She was in profile as she refiled manila folders, unaware that she was being watched. She had on a pair of blue jeans that gave her derriere just the right roundness, and a simple brown crew neck T-shirt that hugged her breasts enough to make his palms itch to follow the same curves.

Her chocolate-colored hair was twisted at the back of her head and pinned so that there was a spray of curls at her crown. Pulled back like that, it left the fresh, natural perfection of her face unconcealed. It struck him that she had a gorgeous neck—slightly long and thin—and that glimpse made him want to kiss the entire length of it.

This can't be good, he told himself, marveling at what the mere sight of her was doing to him.

Northbridge, the people in it and life here were stifling and limiting and restrictive, he reminded himself. He'd been desperate to get away and it was a mistake to be drawn back in. Especially by or for a small-town girl, when not even women who *should* have been able to hold his interest could. Like Celeste, he'd broken away from all this place meant. Unlike his grandmother, he didn't want back in.

But he was here now, he couldn't help thinking. Mara was only a few yards away. And for the life of him, he just didn't have the power to make himself move unless it meant getting to see more of her. To hear her voice. To talk to her. To smell the spring scent of her. Maybe even getting to touch her or kiss her again…

No, nobody who knew him would believe he was acting this way.

He didn't believe it.

He definitely didn't understand it.

But still there was no keeping himself from taking the three steps to the dry cleaner's alley door, raising his bare knuckles to it and knocking.

The last thing Mara expected at ten o'clock on Friday night as she finished her paperwork was to hear a knock on the back door of the dry cleaners.

But after her initial shock, she wasn't afraid. She thought her visitor was most likely Celeste. So without any trepidation at all, she went through the sorting room and opened the door.

To Jared.

Mara had gone to bed on Thursday night still swathed in the wonders of the kiss Jared had left her with. But in the light of day on Friday she'd been brought back to reality. Not only the reality that she should steer clear of Jared Perry, but also the reality that for whatever his reasons, he wasn't altogether glad to be attracted to her. He kept letting her know that he was trying to get her out of his thoughts— he'd kissed her the first time in an attempt to stop thinking about kissing her, and not being able to stop thinking about her, even though he'd apparently been trying, had been a recurring theme the night before, too.

So, okay, fine, Mara had decided. He didn't want to think about her or be attracted to her or distracted with thoughts of kissing her, and she knew without a doubt that he was bad news—going their separate ways was for the best. And since she was behind on her paperwork, that had seemed like a good thing to throw herself into instead.

Only now she'd wrapped up all the paperwork and here he was.

"Oh. Hi," she greeted him, somewhat belatedly and with little enthusiasm.

"Not the warmest welcome I've ever had," he responded.

"I thought maybe Celeste had finally ventured out of her apartment," Mara said as if that explained it. "I wasn't expecting to see you."

"Disappointed?"

I should be that lucky.

But no, despite her cool reception, her heart was beating a mile a minute and every bit of the fatigue she'd been feeling had disappeared the moment she'd looked up into that handsome face.

"No, I'm not disappointed," she assured him. "But I *am* surprised. You keep saying you want to stop thinking about me—that can't happen if you're with me, can it?"

His only answer was a secret smile. Then he nodded in the direction of the upstairs apartment. "I went to see Celeste and noticed the light as I was coming out. I don't know why I didn't notice it going in—probably because I was focused on the idea that you might be at the apartment when I got there. Anyway, when I noticed the light just now I thought

I'd knock and see if I could get the grand tour of your enterprise."

"Am I ripe for takeover?"

His smile stretched into a wicked grin. "I'd better not comment on that one," he said, clearly putting a lascivious spin on her question.

Mara laughed. "You're bad." But she was still disinclined to make this easy for him. "I don't know, maybe I shouldn't let you in. Maybe I should aid the cause and send you home to work more on not thinking about me."

He was undaunted. "Wouldn't help. Nothing does. I even dreamed about you last night."

"Really? What did you dream?"

"That all I wanted to do was have a look at this business that's kept you from finding your soul mate, and you just left me out in the cold."

Mara rolled her eyes.

Jared wasn't wearing The Coat tonight. Instead he had on the first pair of jeans she'd seen on him since his arrival in Northbridge. Jeans that hugged his hips and only hinted at the thickness of the thighs underneath them. He also had on a cream-colored, cable-knit turtleneck sweater that made his chest look massive, and a short, baby-soft-looking black leather jacket that gave him a sexy, bad-boy appeal. Especially with his hands slung in the pockets and his wide shoulders at a cocky angle.

And even though Mara knew she should, she just couldn't resist him.

She stepped out of the doorway so he could come in. "I suppose I don't want to be the stuff of nightmares," she said as if his made-up dream had convinced her.

Once inside he pulled a hand out of his coat pocket to close the door behind him. For no reason Mara could fathom, something about the image of that big hand flat against the back door, about the idea that he'd just shut them away together, sent a little tingle through her as if he'd secluded them in a bedroom rather than a dry cleaner.

It was crazy and she shook it off as soon as she recognized what she was thinking.

Jared removed his jacket and draped it over the door handle. Then he faced Mara and said, "Let's have it—I want to see the place."

"Seriously?"

"Seriously."

"Are you patronizing me?"

"I am not," he said, as if he were insulted that she'd asked. "Celeste tells me that you've turned this place into much more than it once was and I want to see your handiwork."

For a moment Mara studied him, but when she didn't see any signs that he was joking, she actually did give him a tour.

Not that there was a whole lot to see, but there *was* more than she'd begun with. She'd bought out the buildings on both sides of the cleaners, knocked through the side walls that had connected them and expanded the simple dry cleaners that had been her mother's creation. It included a self-service Laundromat, an alterations and dressmaking service and a shoe- and leather-repair operation that had turned the small family business into a considerably more profitable concern.

"—and this is where we started," she said when they came full circle to the rear space again. "We call this the sorting room, but it's also where clean clothes are put on hangers, wrapped and hung to be picked up, and where items get folded. This is the folding table," she concluded, leaning against the side of the big metal table that stood at counter-height against one wall.

"You *have* been busy," Jared said.

"I saw a need and a way of building on what was here and I did it."

He hoisted himself to sit on the table—feet dangling, big hands clasped in the open V between wide-spread thighs.

Maybe it went with the jeans, but he seemed more casual and relaxed than he'd been since his return to town. More like the Northbridge native he was. Or at least had been before he'd left it all behind. But either way, it only increased his appeal.

"And now?" he asked. "Do you have plans to open a chain of Pratt Dry Cleaners?"

Mara laughed, but it had a huskier tone to it than it should have—purely the effect he was having on her again. "No, Northbridge is it for me. I mean, I may do other things here—I'm looking into what it would take to add a carpet and upholstery cleaning service, and our dressmaker and leather guy both want to try their hands at clothing and shoe design, so we may branch off into a little boutique. But whatever I do, it'll only be here. This is where my family is, my friends. Where my life is. I'm all about holding things together, so I'll just go on building on this foundation. I don't need to conquer the world."

"Just your corner of it," he said, repeating her offhand comment of the previous night. "It's nice that you're so content here, though," he added quietly, as if it surprised him that he thought so.

"Nice, but not your cup of tea."

He laughed wryly. "Well, I'll admit that as you've been showing me around I've been automatically thinking that if this was something I was taking over I could sell off each service as a separate business, not *Oh boy, a place to have my clothes cleaned in the heart of idyllic Northbridge.*"

"So you are looking at me as a potential takeover," she said facetiously.

"Well…" he mused in what was obviously a teasing tone. "You did say you and your sister and brothers all inherited this along with the house, right?"

"Right."

"With seven family members all owning a piece of it, I *could* come in and try to get each one to sell out to me. I'd keep at it and sweeten the deals in whatever way I needed to until I wore them down one by one. Then, when I owned a majority share—" he wiggled his eyebrows like a nefarious cartoon character "—I'd own you. But no, like I said, it's just automatic for me to look at the whole pie and see where the best places are to cut it and sell it by the slice. That's what I do."

"But you also said the other night that your heart hasn't been in what you do," she reminded.

"I did say that, didn't I?"

"How come?" Mara asked.

"I said it because it's true."

"No, I mean how come your heart hasn't been in what you do lately?"

He took a breath deep enough for his chest and shoulders to stretch the cables of his sweater before he let it out. "I don't know. It used to be a challenge, a hunt to find companies or corporations or businesses ripe for the taking," he said, paraphrasing her earlier words with a wry smile before he went on. "I liked the maneuvering, the strategizing, the repositioning to find the best approach. And the conquest? That was like winning a game. It was another feather in my cap—"

"And a whole lot of money in your bank account."

"That, too. Then there was a sense of accomplishment when I turned things around and made them work—whether in pieces or all together. There was gratification in knowing my way was better, that I could weed out the deadwood that was dragging things down, get rid of it, make improvements. That I could succeed where someone else had failed—"

"Even if it cost jobs or lost somebody the company they'd built?"

"I'm not to blame for the business mistakes anyone makes to get themselves in a vulnerable position. If you did things that alienated siblings so they *wanted* out of ownership of their portions of what you've done here, would that be my fault?"

"No," Mara conceded.

"And if all that you've done meant that you were overextended, that Neily and your brothers were losing because of it and I came in and allowed them to earn back some money rather than taking a total loss, wouldn't that be good for them?"

"Yes."

"And if, when I sold off the shoe- and leather-repair business, I wrote it into the contract that your leather guy was to keep his job, wouldn't that be better for him than if you went under and he was out of work?"

Mara was able to laugh because this was all hypothetical. "You're really making me the heavy here."

"You're the person in power. The decisions are yours to make, the expansions all your doing, right?"

"Right."

"If, because of your decisions and projects and expansions, things go south on the whole, that's your responsibility then, right?"

"Okay, okay, I'm horrible and you're great."

"Not horrible or great. Just you doing your thing at your time and if it fails, my stepping in to do my thing."

"But now you're not getting a charge out of it anymore," she said to remind him of where this conversation started.

"No. And I'm not really sure why," he said.

"Huh."

"What?"

"It just occurred to me that your grandfather doesn't seem to have found a lot of happiness in life. Now your happiness level is dropping and maybe there's some correlation."

She'd struck a nerve and she saw it in the fact that Jared unclasped his hands to grasp the edges of the table with a tight grip as he gave her a dark frown.

"I'm nothing like the Reverend."

"I know you keep saying you identify with Celeste but—"

"Tell me how you think my grandfather and I are anything alike," he dared her.

"In the first place, I said what the two of you *do* have some similarities. But yes, I guess that's because of some similarities in your personalities." Mara paused, then said, "And remember, you said to tell you how I see it."

"I did. And I'm still waiting to hear it."

"Well, the Reverend seems to have a pretty negative view of—"

"Everything and everyone?" Jared supplied.

"Basically," Mara agreed.

"And because of that he's constantly critical and finding fault," Jared pointed out.

"Yes, and he believes he knows how we should all improve—the right way for life to be lived, for people to behave, for things to be done," Mara expanded, to lay the groundwork for her comparison. Then she said, "A takeover is a pretty negative approach—for anyone on the other end of it—but you do it because you're convinced you know how failing businesses or corporations or whatever should be improved—the right way for them to be run."

"Which has been substantiated by my success."

Mara couldn't suppress a smile at his defensiveness. But she continued anyway. "So your grandfather preaches and imposes his values and morals. You impose your business sense. He was heavy-handed about having Celeste and the rest of your family do things his way, and there isn't much that's more heavy-handed than a hostile takeover, which ultimately means things have to be done *your* way. You even sort of came in and took over here—not that I wasn't glad you got Celeste to agree to having a lawyer who was better than the public defender—but you swept in and—"

"Did what needed to be done," he said.

"The point is," Mara said quietly, "you and the Reverend are sure you have the answers. And getting those answers across—or making people comply with what you both think you see more clearly than anyone else—can mean being harsh or hard on those people."

Mara could tell Jared didn't like the analogy, but he didn't refute it. What he did do was get down off the table, grab her under the arms and lift her to sit on it, standing directly in front of her now. She knew it was a show of just how much power he could wield over her, but there was also something a little arousing in it.

When he had her where he wanted her, he raised an eyebrow and said, "You're pretty brave when I've already told you how I could come in here and wipe the mat with you."

"Only if there was dissension in the ranks and there isn't. Neily and my brothers would never sell to you."

"Pretty sure of yourself, aren't you?" he said with a sexy half smile.

"Yep," she said.

"And according to your theory, I'm becoming disenchanted with what I do for a living because what? On some level it reminds me of the Reverend?"

"I don't have a theory, just observations. I'm only saying—for what it's worth—you might be on a path similar to the one your grandfather has followed. It had to do with being negative and tough on other people, but it hasn't made him a jolly guy who's surrounded by friends and family who enjoy his company. And now you're finding something lacking, so maybe you should look at that."

He moved his hands from where they were flat on the table on either side of her to bracket her waist instead. "And maybe I should prove to you just how different I am from the Reverend."

"This wasn't a challenge, you know," Mara said, feeling the heat of his hands through her shirt. And liking it more than she wanted to.

"No, I don't know that this wasn't a challenge. Saying I'm anything like my grandfather is about as much provocation as anyone can ever throw at me."

"Okay, I take it back."

"Too late."

"Well then, at least I've given you something to think about that isn't me," she goaded.

Jared laughed and Mara liked the sound of *that* more than she wanted to.

"That whole thinking-about-you thing is really bothering you, isn't it?" he goaded in return.

"It isn't bothering me, no," she said loftily, as if she were above the issue. "I'm just trying to give you a break."

He laughed again. "Thanks."

"You're welcome," she said as if his gratitude hadn't been sarcastic.

"But I don't think it's working," he added, as his cool blue eyes looked into hers.

"Maybe you should try hypnosis," she said when it struck her that those eyes of his had almost that effect on her.

"Maybe," he allowed in a quiet, faraway tone just

before he tipped his head to the left and came near enough to give her the barest of kisses. And then a second. And a third.

"Or maybe I should just embrace it," he whispered, so close his words were tufts of sweet air she felt and heard at the same time.

Then one hand came to the side of her neck, his thumb traced the line of her jaw to raise her face just enough for his mouth to take hers completely while his other hand cradled her head.

Mara knew she should probably have been drumming up all the reasons why she shouldn't do this again and stop it. But she didn't. She'd been dying for it for the last twenty-four hours and all she could think was, *Finally...*

So, as lips parted and his tongue came to toy with hers, she raised her hands, too—one to the thick column of his neck and the other to a broad shoulder.

He stepped nearer to the table, nudging her knees apart to accommodate him and then wrapping an arm around her to pull her up against him.

There was nothing shy about the man, and, at that moment, Mara was short on timidity herself. She coursed her fingers up into his hair to test the bristles at his nape and let her other hand drop to the muscles of his back, doing a little closing of the distance herself.

Good grief, could he kiss! But it was more than merely the way he kissed, something happened inside her the instant their lips met. It was as if a warm, bright light went on, casting everything outside of the two of them into shadow.

Both of his arms were around her, his hands massaged her back and she was putty in them. It brought her breasts to the honed wall of his chest where hardened nipples gave a greeting of their own and made Mara suddenly very aware of them. Aware, too, of a need to be even closer to him, to know the feel of his skin, to learn if he was as taut and toned as he seemed through his clothes, and what her touch might do to him.

She drew both of her arms in, ducked them under his elbows and then slid her hands beneath the hem of his sweater.

Satin over steel—that initial feel of his back was almost luxurious. Mara scaled the heights of it, to reach massive shoulders any weight lifter would have envied.

His mouth had opened even wider in response to her touch, deepening the kiss, upping the intimacy and giving her a little secret delight to know she could have this effect on him. His tongue grew more insistent and aggressive, but Mara's kept up with him, carried away by that kiss, by having his bare flesh beneath her palms, her taut nipples pressed against him.

His hand at her back began to travel, too, dipping to her waist where it had started out, inching under her T-shirt to her bare skin.

It wasn't a callused hand, but it was all male: strong and not too smooth, unhesitating as he slid up at a pace slow enough to give warning but that showed no signs of caution.

Mara fought not to writhe in anticipation and because it felt so fabulous to have his hand on *her* bare skin, and when that hand closed around the lacy cup of her bra she lost a little of the battle and took a deep breath that pushed her breast into his grasp.

The bra was her enemy then. She didn't want his touch filtered and the lace did just that.

But thankfully not for long before he slipped his hand inside.

Masterful and possessive, he molded that tender globe, kneading, massaging, teasing, exploring as her nipple curled into his palm as if that was where it belonged. Until his fingers found it, gently plucking it like a strand of saffron from the heart of the crocus flower, circling it, testing it, turning it into a tiny pebble of delight that awakened other parts of her.

Parts much lower and suddenly right up against that part of Jared—the solid ridge behind the zipper of his jeans—that was letting her know she was not alone in the desires growing with each passing moment.

Then Jared leaned forward slightly, enough to let her know that he was aiming to lay her down on that table.

He'd join her there, she knew. And it would find a whole new use beyond folding shirts.

But while there was terrible, terrible temptation to let him do just that, Mara's mind also skipped ahead to what would happen when this moment passed. When she was here again only for business, when he was long gone and all she had left to remember him by was a silver work table.

Because that *would* be all she'd have left, she reminded herself. Jared Perry might be here now—in all his glory—but she knew there was no way he was staying much longer. And she wondered if she would be sorry. If every day she would come to work, look at that table, remember and regret...

And Mara didn't do things she was afraid she might regret.

So, rather than cooperate and allow Jared to lay her back, she drew her hands around to his front and held him at bay.

It cost her dearly.

His hand abandoned her breast and dropped to her side again.

His tongue did a last turn around hers and disappeared.

His openmouthed kiss ended, replaced by a more chaste one before that stopped, too.

"No fooling around in the workplace," he said then, letting her know he'd gotten the idea.

"How could I ever fold choir robes on this table again?" she joked, her own voice almost as husky as his, but not quite.

Jared sighed, looked into her eyes and then kissed her again—long and deep and soundly enough that, for a moment, Mara forgot why she hadn't merely given in to what her whole body was aching for.

But then he ended that kiss, too, pulled his hand out completely from under her shirt, caught her under the arms and lifted her off the table.

Then he took a step back, jutted a hip out to brace his weight against the table's edge and said, "Have dinner with me tomorrow night."

She hadn't expected the invitation. Her first thought was that he believed the only thing that had kept her from making love with him tonight was the place, that if he took her out, if they had a real date, it might end differently than this had.

So, she shook her head. "I have plans," she said, glad it was true because she wasn't too sure she would have been able to say no otherwise.

"Plans for what?"

"Dinner. There's a group of us who do a progressive meal once a month—"

"A progressive meal?"

"Everyone makes one course, we go from house to house, eat that course, then go on to the next house and the next course. I'm dessert."

That made him smile a smile as deliciously evil as she'd ever seen, and she knew exactly what he was thinking.

"You could let me be your date," he said.

"Even if I did, that doesn't mean you'd be getting

anything more than cheesecake for dessert," she informed him.

He nodded that deadly handsome head of his. "Not why I asked you out, but understood. I really only wanted to have dinner with you tomorrow night."

Mara studied him, wondering if that were true. Almost hoping it wasn't. Not completely, at any rate.

Then he smiled yet another kind of smile—endearing and sexy and mischievous all rolled into one—and said, "Come on. Or aren't you allowed to bring anyone?"

"It's mostly couples and yes, dates are allowed," she heard herself admit as she thought of how many times she'd been to one of these dinners alone and wished she wasn't. "But you might be bored out of your mind—it *is* only a bunch of us bumpkins getting together for dinner."

"So I'll get the chance to see people I haven't seen since I left town," he countered. Then he leaned forward and said, "Don't small-town manners dictate that now that I've invited myself you act as if you'd wanted me to come all along?"

"Will you behave?"

"Like the Reverend's grandson that I am."

That made her smile and give in. Because, after all, she wanted to be with him in spite of knowing better.

"All right. Be at my house at six."

He kissed her again, playfully, and headed for

the door. "Six," he confirmed as he shrugged into his leather jacket. "And you're not on the dessert menu," he added just before he opened the alley door and went out.

Mara watched as he passed in front of the window near the door and headed away from the dry cleaners. Once she knew he was truly gone she couldn't resist turning and pressing a hand to the cold metal of the table where she'd been sitting moments before.

Maybe she shouldn't have stopped him, she thought as her pulse still raced and her breasts still strained against the confines of her bra, and her entire body seemed to yearn for what she could have had.

No, it was better that she hadn't let things go any further, she told herself.

But even though that seemed true on every rational, reasonable level, it was difficult to buy when wanting him so badly was a thrumming need beating through her.

And no matter what she'd just told him about cheesecake being the only thing he was going to get for dessert the next night, she wasn't altogether sure she'd be able to stick to it.

Chapter Eight

"I have to say that that was *nothing* like what I thought it would be," Jared said.

Mara had just seen her last guest to the door after the progressive dinner Saturday night and rejoined Jared in the living room where empty dessert plates, wineglasses and cappuccino cups were scattered everywhere.

"What did you think it would be like?" she asked as she sat on the sofa with him, angling her body so they were facing each other.

"I don't know. It's Northbridge. I thought pot roast or fried chicken and mashed potatoes, or barbecue and beer. Or—worst-case scenario— potluck tuna casserole. And nothing but talk about whose hatchet throwing had won first prize at the fair and how it had caused a feud with someone else."

"And instead you had imported olives, herbed goat cheese and breaded eggplant appetizers, roasted butternut squash soup with crème fraiche and pancetta, wilted wild greens salad with warm bacon dressing and feta, elk strips with green and red peppers, braised vegetables, homemade bread baked in the Newtons' new wood-burning pizza oven—"

"And that cheesecake," he finished rapturously. "That was like nothing I've ever had. Tell me again what it was."

"Cherry chocolate cheesecake mousse."

"Plus the wines and liqueurs were some of the best and paired impeccably to each course—"

"Thanks to Tom Hawks, our resident wine connoisseur."

"I can honestly say that I've never had a meal as good anywhere in the world," Jared concluded.

Mara couldn't suppress a smile she knew had to be smug. "Thanks to the Internet the world has come to Northbridge. But the nice part about it is that there hasn't had to be any real invasion—it's our best-kept secret. Well, that and who won the hatchet-throwing competition and caused a feud," she finished facetiously.

"Okay, no, I wasn't bored the way I was afraid I might be but—"

"I know—this *is* Northbridge, so how could I

blame you for worrying that the hayseeds wouldn't be able to keep you interested?"

"Last night it was bumpkins, tonight hayseeds—I want it noted that those are *your* terms, not mine."

"So that *isn't* how you think of those of us who stayed here rather than going out into the great beyond?" Mara challenged.

Jared's grin was higher on one side than the other. "That *was* how I thought of the populace of North-bridge. But to be fair, when I lived here a progressive dinner really would have been potluck with a variety of tuna casseroles as the main draw. But now, obviously, *progressive* means more than walking from house to house. Which I enjoyed. It means the food and conversation are progressive, too," he added, as if that surprised him as well. "It was fun. And good to see everybody. I didn't know the group would be so large."

"We started out smaller but couldn't keep it that way. And actually, it works out well because now we rotate the cooking so for every one time I have a course to prepare, I get to go to the next two dinners and just eat."

"And not clean up afterward," Jared noted with a glance at the dishes. Then he stood and said, "Come on, I'll help you with these."

Mara watched him for a moment as he began to gather dessert debris, drinking in the sight of him as she had all evening.

Tonight he had on a pair of dark, charcoal-colored

wool slacks that caressed his narrow hips and rear end in praise of what was beneath them, and a black turtleneck sweater that—while not overly tight—still left little to the imagination when it came to the width of his shoulders, his bulging biceps and his honed pectorals, which she wished she'd learned the feel of the night before when she'd had her hands under his shirt.

As far as she was concerned, he'd been the best-looking man there tonight, and every time she'd glanced at him something was set atwitter inside her.

Belatedly she got to her feet again to pitch in, collecting plates, silverware, glasses and mugs.

"It did seem as if you were having a good time," she said then. "I still can't believe you knew Joshua Cantrell. If that isn't proof that it's a small world, I don't know what is."

"I sold him a shoe factory, which was part of a footwear conglomerate I took over. That's a perfect example of what I was talking about before. He benefited because he got a factory he needed as the tennis-shoe tycoon, and he put the people who had been employed by the previous owner back to work. All positive results."

Mara agreed by raising an empty port glass as if in toast. "And the two of you meet again here."

"With him married to Cassie Walker and living in Northbridge most of the time now, it *is* a small world," Jared agreed. Then, as they took everything into the kitchen, he said, "It was good to see Chloe Carmichael and Reid Walker again, too. I'm glad they could overcome her snooty parents' disapproval and their past to get together again. And Clair Cabot married to Ben Walker—the Reverend was convinced Ben was going to end up in jail and instead here he is, running that school for delinquent boys and about to become a father in a couple of months."

"And every one of them happy in Northbridge, of all places," Mara couldn't resist goading.

The dirty dishes were in the sink and before she could tackle them she said, "Ugh! I have to get out of these boots, they're killing me."

She bent over to unzip the knee-high footwear and slipped them off.

When she'd accomplished that and straightened up again, she caught Jared staring.

The boot removal had not been designed to wow him, but she had chosen the dress she was wearing with that in mind. It was a brown sweater-knit number that followed her every curve to midcalf length. The V-neck was edged with knit ruffles that crossed the bust to end at the side of her waist and was so deeply cut that she'd almost considered wearing something under the dress to fill it in. In the end she hadn't, though, and it was in the direction of that plunging neckline that Jared's gaze had landed.

At least until he averted it because, true to his word, he was on his best behavior. He hadn't deliv-

ered a single innuendo, suggestive comment or so
much as an untoward glance until then.

His grandfather would have been proud.

Mara had been slightly disappointed.

But now she was gratified to discover that he
wasn't totally unaffected by her, especially since
she'd paid special attention to her blush, eye shadow
and mascara, and taken extra care with her hair so it
was a sleek, shiny curtain falling freely to her shoulders where it curved under on the ends.

She hid a smile and began to rinse the dishes.

"So this is it for you," Jared said then. "You're not
here because you got stuck with the family business
or just never got around to leaving or were afraid to
go out on your own or something. You genuinely like
living in Northbridge. You're not only content, you're
perfectly satisfied with your life just the way it is."

"I do like it here, yes," Mara answered with a
laugh at how foreign he seemed to find that concept.
"As for perfectly satisfied with my life? I'm satisfied to be living in Northbridge, but it's not as if I
don't want *anything* to change."

"The business expansions you talked about last
night," he guessed.

"More than that. I'd like to get married again—
not to another jerk who takes off, but to someone
who will stick around, who I can have a family
with."

"A family you raise in Northbridge," he said, still
with a certain amount of distaste.

"You really have to stop blaming Northbridge for the way your life was when *you* lived here. It wasn't the town that held you under its thumb, it was the Reverend. For me it was and is a great place. It's safe and cheery and friendly. It's like a big family that, for the most part, gets along and cares about each other and looks out for each other and wants what's best for everyone else. What better place to have and raise a family?"

Jared was watching her closely as she loaded the dishwasher, studying her as if he were trying to figure her out, and yet still his eyes on her raised her temperature considerably.

Trying to ignore that, Mara glanced at him and decided to venture into something that had occurred to her but that she hadn't been sure she would actually say to him. "I've been thinking about some of the things you've said…"

"Uh-huh."

"You think it's so weird that anyone has stayed in Northbridge, let alone that we might be happy about it and want to go on living here. But when it comes to yourself, you aren't sure love or marriage or commitment are for you—I'm assuming that means you don't see having kids in your future…."

She left that dangling, waiting for him to tell her if she was right or wrong.

"It isn't that I don't like kids," he said. "Or that I've sworn never to have them. I just… Well, I've never thought about having them either."

"So where your career was the be all and end all for you, now it's not giving you that kind of buzz anymore. If you never have a family to focus on and fill your life, and your job isn't thrilling you, what *do* you see for yourself in the future? Forty cats penned up in a penthouse apartment so you have something to come home to, and searching out antique butter churns you can outbid old ladies for at auctions to keep you in the hunt-and-conquest mode?"

He laughed. "Are you telling me that you see my future as bleak?"

"I'm just asking how *you* see it," she said as she closed the dishwasher. "Or what you have planned for it."

"I'll tell you what I *don't* have planned for it— that outbidding-old-ladies-for-butter-churns thing or buying forty cats," he said. But still he seemed to consider her question about what he *did* see in his future.

Then he said, "I haven't really thought much about 'what now,' to tell you the truth. I know I certainly wasn't thinking that what was ahead for me was bleak—at least not until you had me living with forty cats and beating out old ladies at auctions to get a few kicks. But I will say that I came here feeling…I don't know, unstimulated, I guess. And I'll admit that I expected that after being here everything else would seem exciting as hell again."

"In comparison to the horrible tedium you were convinced would be Northbridge."

"Tedium, stuffiness, self-righteousness, small-mindedness—"

"Again, that's the Reverend, not Northbridge."

"Which is why I guess even though I haven't developed a *bleak* outlook for my future, I am a little surprised to find that in comparison to what I'm seeing in you and Joshua Cantrell and the Walker brothers and other people around here, I'm willing to concede that something might be missing—another dimension—and I'm not so sure that what I'll go home to *will* seem fulfilling again in comparison."

Mara laughed once more. "That's as much as you'll concede—that you were hoping Northbridge would be so awful that once you'd had another taste of it, it would give you a new lease on your old life. But it isn't quite awful enough to accomplish that?"

"How much would you have me concede?" he asked with a healthy dose of mischief, raised eyebrows and all.

"Admit that you're seeing Northbridge through new eyes now and that you might even like it. Just a tiny, tiny bit."

He leaned forward far enough to reach for her arm and bring her closer.

"I like some of what Northbridge has to offer," he said with a suggestive twinkle in his pale-blue eyes that let her know he was referring to her.

Mara purposely misinterpreted. "Excellent cooks, stimulating company, a calm, peaceful lifestyle," she said instead, listing what Northbridge had to offer.

"And you," he said, not letting her get away with ignoring his intentions.

"If Northbridge is offering me for something it better not be for anything but dry cleaning," she joked.

Jared laughed again and pulled her even nearer, kissing her playfully, in keeping with the tone at that moment.

But for Mara that kiss was like a cool, clear glass of the purest water on a hot, dry day—it was all she'd been thinking about since the night before, what she'd been thirsty for the entire evening.

It ended too soon and she was unhappy.

"I'd probably better get going then, since I don't need any dry cleaning."

Oh. So he was taking her offhand comment as a message. And coupled with her warning of the previous night that having dinner with her tonight was not to be a route to finishing what they'd started, he no doubt believed he was respecting her wishes.

And now she was wishing that hadn't been the message she'd given.

"We aren't at the dry cleaners," she heard herself respond, having no idea what it was supposed to mean but at a loss for anything else to say.

"No, we aren't," Jared agreed with a small, secret smile. "But I've had my slice of cheesecake and, as I recall, I was told that was the extent of it for me tonight."

"That was what you were told," Mara confirmed.

"And I'm just trying to play by the rules."

"An admirable policy."

"Even if I don't want to," he added, kissing her again and weakening her knees and her will even more.

"It's probably what we should do, though," Mara said when that kiss ended, her lack of enthusiasm for following her own rules clear in her voice.

"Probably," Jared conceded, tilting his head to kiss her neck this time, to nibble her earlobe. "I know I don't want to," he whispered then. "But I'm on your turf and I'll do whatever you say—stay if you say stay, go if you say go…"

She didn't suppose she was indicating he should go by tipping her head to one side, giving him easier access to her neck. But even as she did, even as she nearly wilted beneath the feel of the feathery brushes of his lips, she was considering what she should— or shouldn't—do.

He *was* on her turf, but he wouldn't be forever and that was something she had to think about, she told herself. If she did this, it didn't mean a beginning for them. It was only about tonight and she knew it.

It was just that she wanted tonight. She wanted him. So much she couldn't fight it.

After all, he was the most remarkable man she'd ever known, the only man who had made her blood rush the way it was at that moment. The only man who might ever make her feel the way she did right now. If she accepted that *right now* was all she would have of him, why *couldn't* she have it?

There might have been solid reasons why she

couldn't—or shouldn't. But the more he kissed her neck, the more his warm breath bathed her skin, the more she wanted to simply indulge. Like a once-in-a-lifetime vacation to an exotic place she'd never be able to go to again—it was still worth it to go once, wasn't it?

"Stay," she said in a voice so quiet it was a mere sigh.

Jared didn't need it to be louder, though. And he didn't say anything in answer to it, he just kissed a line up her neck to her jaw, her chin and her lower lip before he recaptured her mouth completely.

His lips parted over hers and just the tip of his tongue began to trace the inner edges of her teeth, taking his time coming to greet her tongue. But eventually he got there, doing a sexy circle around it to entice it out onto the dance floor.

Mara's arms went around him and her breasts came into contact with his chest. Her nipples were already taut with memories of what it had been like to have his hands there the previous evening, with the need to have them back.

His arms came around her, too, but low on her hips, not quite on her rear end but almost. Yet, even as her body started to awaken, she was still enmeshed in that kiss. That wonderful kiss that he did so well she wanted it to last for hours and hours.

Really, it wasn't merely technique that made each one special, though, she realized as lips opened wider and tongues toyed with each other brashly and unabashedly. There was something about how their mouths fitted together, how their tongues met, how his biceps rode hers—possessed hers—that made it seem almost as if it was all designed to come together. And it left her wondering if that would be the case for more than kissing…

The kiss came to a conclusion then. But only so that Jared could kiss the other side of her neck, following a downward path now with soft, scant brushes of his lips, of his tongue against her skin all the way to the V of her dress.

"Show me which room is yours," he encouraged, his words hot licks against her suddenly tingling flesh.

And while Mara knew this was yet another chance for her to rethink her decision, she didn't do it. She just took his hand to lead him up the back stairs to the house's second floor.

There were no lights on and Mara didn't change that, turning instead to face Jared, to drink in the sight of his achingly handsome face in the white moon glow coming through her bedroom window.

Jared didn't complain. He only pulled her close again and took her mouth with a greater hunger, wider and more demanding as though something was being unleashed inside him, something that infected Mara, too.

She slipped her hands under his sweater to his back again, working that muscular expanse with palms and fingertips, absorbing the feel of him, the sleekness of him.

The image of how he'd looked all evening in that black sweater appeared in her mind's eye and she recalled wishing that she had paid attention the night before to more than his bare back. So, now that she had her second opportunity, she did some exploring, bringing her hands around to his front.

His pectorals were equally as developed as the rest of him, and she reveled in making his male nipples stand almost as taut as her own were.

While one of his hands braced her back, the other came around to her breast, and tonight the fact that he started on the outside of her dress made for a double offense; her thin, lacy bra and the lightweight sweaterdress might as well have been armor for all the barrier they provided between her straining breasts and his hand.

Jared must not have been any more satisfied than she was with the conditions because he slid both hands under the shoulders of her neckline, easing the dress off so that it fell to her feet.

Transparent bra, thong and thigh-high nylons were what she had on underneath, but standing there in the moonlight made her determined that she not be the only one of them that vulnerable. So Mara sluiced her hands upward to his shoulders, bringing his sweater with her and breaking off their kiss to pull it over his head, then toss it aside.

Once she had, she didn't seek out his mouth again immediately. For a moment she looked at his naked torso, which was even better than she'd expected. Massive chest and shoulders, carved and cut arms, perfect pectorals and abs tight enough for her fingers to skip across as though they were harp strings.

Since what had waited for her under his sweater had been so much better than she'd anticipated, she couldn't help wondering if what was waiting under his slacks might prove more impressive, too. Especially when she could feel the firm ridge of arousal against her stomach. And not only did she not want to be the only one of them undressed, now she was driven to know what other treasures lay beneath the rest of his expertly tailored clothes.

She found the hook above his zipper, unfastened it, and then drew the zipper itself down. From there his burgeoning desire for her was evident behind his boxers.

Jared was a step ahead of her, though, remembering his shoes and—after taking protection from his pocket—shedding everything from the waist down with more ease than she could have managed.

And then, there he was, completely naked before her, and the magnificence of him took her breath away.

Which sounded like a small gasp when he swept her up into his arms, swung her onto the downy quilt of her queen-sized bed and then joined her there.

His mouth came to hers with a new urgency as he filled his hand with her breast for only a few minutes before he unclasped her bra and flung it away.

It was so much better then! Having his warm,

adept hand caressing the engorged globe was no less than divine.

Or maybe it was because, when his mouth deserted hers to replace his hand on her breast, that was even better.

Such dark, hot sweetness…

She drew her hands along the breadth of his shoulders. Working his flesh, too, she was barely aware that he was divesting her of thong and nylons so that nothing whatsoever stood between them.

Then it was only delicious delight.

His mouth was a marvel: sucking, licking, nipping, tugging at breast and nipple. The desire built inside her as his hands coursed over every inch of her and then glided from the top of her thigh to her inner thigh and up, reaching between her legs.

That first touch of her center made him moan as if he'd found nirvana, but Mara was so enmeshed in the magic he was working that she couldn't breathe at all.

She was on her back with Jared on his side. His incredible body was partially atop hers, his leg was across hers, and that long, thick shaft of steel was at her hip, making her more and more aware of it, more and more aware of the craving for it that was on the verge of consuming her.

She reached for him, giving a little of what she was receiving at the same time she was learning the full extent of that last frontier of masculine majesty before it was sheathed.

Then, suddenly, Jared was above her, between her legs, his weight braced on powerful arms.

He dipped down to kiss her, his tongue thrusting in and out, giving her a preview of what was to come. Then he penetrated her with slow, measured intent.

She pushed her hips toward him as she watched the unutterable glory of the man himself, of chiseled features carved with passion, of muscles tensed to their limit and glistening in the moonlight.

Wanting more of him, Mara slid her palms from his straining shoulders down bulging pectorals to his sides, savoring the taut, honed feel of him as he finally embedded himself within her.

She clasped his sculpted derriere with insistent hands, bringing her legs up and around his, welcoming him with a raise of her hips that seated him within her as flawlessly as their mouths had met before.

But this flawless joining was made even better by him drawing out and coming back, each return driving him farther into her, deeper and deeper.

In the same way her legs were entwined with his, she wound her arms around the pillars that were his arms on either side of her. Clinging to his shoulders, she moved with him, meeting him thrust for thrust at an ever-increasing speed, staying with him while need grew gargantuan.

Her eyes closed as she was consumed with what was happening inside, as the heat and power of him infused her, driving her to higher reaches until she burst through to the top in an explosion that was exquisite and earthshaking, bright enough to be blinding, hot enough to meld them togethe and profound in a way that made it seem as if there, with him, she'd discovered something greater than she'd ever imagined existed.

Just then his powerful hips seized, the small of his back curved and he plunged even deeper into her, exploding himself, frozen at his own zenith as their bodies seemed to fuse and his carried hers to soar higher still, leaving her incapable of anything but hanging on as absolute, sheer and utter ecstasy held her in its grip.

Then everything began to ease. Only a little at a time. Inch by inch. Ounce by ounce.

Mara was suddenly aware of the pounding of her heart. Jared's elbows bent, he lowered his upper half to hers, and she could feel his pulse beating in answer to hers. His breath was steamy against her ear and her breath was steamy bouncing off his shoulder. And while the weight of him pushed her into the quilt beneath her, it felt as if they were cushioned by a cloud.

Jared flexed within her, reminding her that their bodies had not yet parted and she liked that, too.

"Can I still stay?" he asked in a raspy voice.

She wasn't sure if he meant could he stay inside her or could he stay the night. It didn't matter. The answer was the same for both.

"Yes."

Apparently he'd meant could he stay the night because he slipped out of her then and rolled to his back beside her. But just when she was worried she was going to lose what she wanted most at that moment—to be held by him, to be as close to him as possible—he pulled her to lie so near she was partly on top of him, using his chest as a pillow.

Then he yanked the edge of the quilt to more than cover them both. He pulled it so tightly around them that they were cocooned by it, and wrapped his arms so firmly around her within the cocoon that she didn't think she could have escaped if she'd wanted to. Although she definitely didn't want to.

"I'm not sure what's going on here, Small Town, but something is," he whispered.

Mara didn't answer him. She wasn't exactly sure *how* to answer him.

But she was sure of one thing—something *was* going on between them. Something that seemed outside of them both. Bigger than them both. Stronger.

She just had to remind herself that, in spite of that, she was not likely to have more than this night with him.

And while she was reasonably sure that wasn't going to be enough for her in the long run, right then, in his arms, with their satiated bodies molded together, it was just about as good as it could get.

Chapter Nine

Jared had been asleep with Mara still in his arms when the call had come in on his cell phone Sunday morning that the Reverend was well enough and ready to talk.

It had made for a hasty goodbye that he regretted, but he hadn't had any other option. The Reverend had decreed that everyone—authorities, family and even Celeste herself—be present for his statement. Considering that his grandfather was making it a somewhat public forum, Jared had seized the opportunity to have Stephanie there, as well. Just in case. But that had meant he needed to make immediate arrangements to fly Stephanie into Billings, and he'd had to do some fancy footwork to put the meeting off long enough for Celeste's lawyer to arrive.

Mara had opted not to attend since Jared could offer Celeste support and because it had seemed to be a Perry family event. But at four o'clock that afternoon the elderly Reverend's hospital room was filled to the brim with an array of onlookers gathered to hear what he had to say.

Jared stood near the foot of the hospital bed with Celeste and Stephanie, thinking how much his grandfather loved an audience. But he kept his opinion to himself, just as he was keeping most of what he thought about his grandfather to himself so that nothing got in the way of what he hoped would put an end to the proceedings against Celeste.

"Because it seems that I can be silent no longer, I've asked that everyone be here for this so that I don't have to repeat myself," the elderly man announced. "I'll go through it all one time and one time only, and then I will never speak of it again. To anyone." Having said that—and sitting ramrod straight in his hospital bed—the Reverend looked expectantly to the district attorney, the state police investigator and the FBI agent at his bedside.

"Can you tell us where you were at approximately midnight on the night the Northbridge Bank was robbed in 1960?" the D.A. asked.

"I was at the old north bridge, having followed my *wife* to finally confront her with the fact that she was being unfaithful, to try to talk her into stopping her sordid behavior, repent and work harder at being the dutiful wife and mother she should have been."

That had been aimed at Celeste, and Jared was fairly certain that his grandfather had requested her presence so that he could castigate her in front of everyone. But Celeste merely absorbed it, showing no emotion.

"What did you find when you arrived at the bridge?" the FBI agent asked.

"Events much worse than I had expected. I came upon my *wife* at the center of an argument between two men who, it quickly became apparent, had robbed the Northbridge Bank."

"Was there any indication that Celeste Perry— your wife—had participated in that robbery?" the same man inquired.

"No," the Reverend said without hesitation but also as if he were sorry to have to admit it. "It was very clear that she was shocked and appalled to learn that that was what had been done. She'd clearly had no part in it."

"What were the men arguing about?"

"Celeste. Her lover wanted to bring her along when they fled, his partner did not."

"And did your wife voice her preference?"

"She was disinclined to go when she learned what they'd done."

"And where were you at this time?" the state investigator asked.

"I was in the bushes, where I couldn't be seen,

so that I could see the lay of the land before I announced myself. I'd heard raised voices as I'd approached the bridge and thought it best to know what I might be getting into ahead of time."

"So the men were arguing," the D.A. prompted.

"They were. And then they got into a physical fight, one of them was pushed backward, fell and hit his head. He died instantly."

"Was Celeste involved in that fight or the push that resulted in the man's death?"

"No." Again unhesitatingly and begrudgingly, as if he wished he could respond differently. "She was shouting for them to stop, but she wasn't anywhere near the brawl."

"And after it was determined that the man was dead?" the state investigator inquired.

"Her lover dragged the body into the woods to bury him. And while he was otherwise occupied, I came forward," the Reverend said, his bony chin rising and his tone and expression revealing how distasteful he found it to be talking about this.

"What happened then?"

"I debased myself by asking her to honor her obligations to me and to her sons by coming home."

The Reverend glared at Celeste with what Jared thought was unmistakable hatred even after all these years.

Then the older man continued. "She had difficulty making the correct choice and before we could escape, her lover returned to the bridge."

"Frank Dorian," the police investigator supplied.

The Reverend confirmed it only by not denying it before he went on. "At that point I became a liability because he realized that I knew not only about the robbery, but also that he'd been instrumental in his partner's death. He decided that I should join his partner."

"In what respect?" the investigator asked for clarification.

"He was going to kill me as well," the elderly man answered bluntly. "That was when my *dear* wife did possibly the only decent thing she'd ever done—she persuaded him against killing me by saying that if he killed me he would have to kill her, too, but that if he allowed me to live she would go away with him after all."

Jared was convinced by the Reverend's tone and demeanor that the words themselves tasted bitter in his grandfather's mouth.

"So Frank Dorian didn't harm you," the D.A. said.

"He took me into the woods and tied me up. I worked the entire night on the ties and only freed myself as the sun was rising. But by the time I returned to town, word had already spread that the bank had been robbed. No one knew yet that Celeste had left."

"Did you report what you knew to the authorities then?" the state investigator asked.

"No," the Reverend responded in a lower tone than he'd yet used.

"You didn't report that you knew who the robbers were, where they'd gone right after the robbery, that one of them had been killed by the other or that your wife had left with the surviving man?" the D.A. asked.

"No."

Jared saw his grandfather's jaw clench and knew how much it galled him to have to say what he was about to.

The elderly man took a deep breath and squared his shoulders belligerently. "I'd suffered a *wife* who had not only carried on with two men at once, she'd done it blatantly, out in the open where everyone— where my *congregation*—could see what she was doing and know she was making a fool of me. I'd tried to turn a blind eye to it in hopes that she would come to her senses, stop it, beg my forgiveness and salvage our family. I'd held my head high and pretended
I didn't know what was being said about both of us—"

He cut himself off, staring venomously at Celeste before raising his chin again and transferring his gaze to the district attorney.

"As you can imagine, her leaving with her lover, choosing a thief, a criminal, over me—"

"But you said that she chose to go with him to save you," the investigator reminded.

"At the bridge. But she'd been choosing that despicable low-life itinerant for all the weeks before that. She'd chosen to leave our home, our sons, that night with every intention of running off with her lover, of deserting us. The fact that the robbery put a sour taste in her mouth at the last minute hardly excused the cuckold she'd made of me before that. To return to town, to be the one to feed the news to everyone I knew, to say *she'd* saved *me?* You can't even imagine the embarrassment, the humiliation, the degradation…"

"So you did nothing," the D.A. said.

"Nothing," the Reverend confirmed. "Not when I thought about what would happen if Celeste and her lover were caught and brought back. I was afraid Celeste could be tried as an accomplice of some sort in the robbery, that there would be even more scandal, more gossip, and that would have added to the harm she'd already done to me and my sons. But if Celeste wasn't captured and brought back, we would have to weather nothing more than the specu-lation and suspicions when everyone learned that she had gone missing the same night the robbery happened. Speculation and suspicion are easier to weather with dignity, faster than fact to die down and be forgotten. So no, I did not speak up."

"And by not speaking up you hid that Mickey Rider was dead and buried in the woods," the inves-tigator pointed out.

"The death of a no-good thief?" the Reverend nearly shouted in outrage. "A death that was acciden-tal in nature? Should I have sacrificed my sons to report that?"

No one answered that question.

Instead the D.A. said, "We've also been told that you were aware that your wife had come back to town as Leslie Vance and still you opted not to reveal any of what you knew."

"Initially I was furious that she had the audacity to slink into Northbridge and live right under my nose," the Reverend said.

"Did you reconsider revealing what you knew?" the investigator asked.

"I fantasized about turning her in. I considered denying that I'd ever been at the bridge that night or knew anything of what had gone on. It would have been her word against mine and whose would hold more water?" he said with relish.

"But you didn't." This from the D.A.

"Again, my name and the names of my sons would have been dragged through the mud. Ten *years* after the fact. We'd passed the worst of the talk about Celeste leaving with the robbers, I didn't want that can of worms reopened."

"So you maintained your silence and suffered her living right under your nose," the D.A. repeated the Reverend's phrase.

"I would have liked to run her out, believe me. But I couldn't do that without bringing attention to who she really was. Besides, I could see from the way she was forced to live—making nothing but hourly wages at the dry cleaners, alone in a tiny apartment—that she hadn't been the recipient of any of the stolen money. I decided that living in fear, a virtual recluse, having to keep to the background like a scared rabbit waiting for the fox to find it, was just punishment for what she'd done."

"And if you'd let it be known who she was, her sons and grandchildren might have been more forgiving than you were. She might have been let into their lives and you wouldn't have wanted that," Jared said, unable to stop himself.

His grandfather stared at him. "Yes," he said maliciously. "I told her I would keep her secret as long as she remained removed from you all—her own family. And I felt a certain amount of vindication—vindication I was due—in the fact that she could only know her own sons, her own grandchildren, from a distance. That she couldn't be involved with the family she regretted leaving. That she could only ever be an outsider looking in. The counter clerk at the dry cleaners and nothing more."

"Or else," Jared said under his breath, completing his grandfather's threat.

"Or else," the Reverend repeated with what sounded like self-satisfaction.

Jared shook his head at the old man, knowing nothing he said would ever change him.

After several more questions to make certain all the bases were covered, the D.A., the FBI agent and the state investigator left the hospital room to confer in the corridor.

"Are you proud of what you've done?" the Reverend asked Celeste when they were gone.

"I'm only sorry for it, Armand," Celeste answered calmly, wearily. "So, so sorry for it all."

"It seems to me that that's a sentiment you might consider sharing," Jared couldn't help saying to the older man, who pretended not to even hear it.

Silence descended on the room then and lasted until the authorities finally returned.

When they did, it was the D.A. who spoke, first to the Reverend.

The district attorney reprimanded Armand severely for withholding information that would have revealed the death of Mickey Rider, and that could have led to the earlier arrest of Frank Dorian and the recovery of the bank's money. It was made clear that the Reverend was considered culpable despite his personal feelings and could have been forced to answer for his lack of action. But considering the amount of time that had passed and the fact that both Frank Dorian and Mickey Rider were no longer living, the reprimand was all that would be leveled against the older man.

The D.A. told the room in general that the FBI was displeased to have to accept that none of the money from the bank robbery had been recovered, but because their investigation had turned up no evidence that Celeste either had the money or had ever benefited from it, they were not pursuing any avenue against her.

Lastly, since what the Reverend had said had corroborated Celeste's story, the state investigator and the D.A. were in agreement that she not be charged or tried in the death of Mickey Rider.

"In conclusion," the district attorney announced, "both the case of the bank robbery and the death of Mickey Rider will now be considered closed."

Luckily Noah was on the other side of Celeste because when she heard that, she wilted and it took both Jared and his brother to keep the rotund woman from hitting the floor.

"You're sure you aren't dizzy anymore?" Jared asked Celeste.

She'd been very quiet since she'd fainted at the hospital, saying next to nothing all the way back to Northbridge and even through the take-out dinner they'd just finished at her apartment late Sunday night.

"I'm fine," his grandmother assured, still sounding melancholy. "It's just been a long day and I guess I'm a little out of whack."

"I'm sure," Jared said, thinking that it had been more than a long day for Celeste. It had been a long haul—forty-seven years of staying under the radar and pretending to be someone else.

But he had every confidence that given some time, everything would be all right. After being revived from her swoon and getting out of the Reverend's hospital room, Celeste had had a short visit with her sons and the grandchildren who had come to hear the Reverend's statement to the authorities. Most of the grandchildren had already paid calls on Celeste at her apartment, but since Jared's father and uncle lived in Billings, today was the first time they'd been face-to-face with the woman they'd known as the clerk at the hometown dry cleaners and who they now knew was really their long-lost mother.

The reunion had gone well, though, Jared thought. His father and uncle held no grudges against their mother and had made that clear to her. But still Jared was aware of how physically and emotionally exhausting the entire ordeal had been for Celeste, who was going to have to come to grips with living openly again and adjust to being able to associate with the family she'd only been allowed to view from a distance most of her life. It was no wonder she was a little out of whack.

From where Jared was sitting on the couch, he poured Celeste another glass of the brandy she liked.

She thanked him and then she said, "I suppose you'll be leaving town now."

"I thought I'd stay through the week—until after Eden's wedding next Saturday anyway. Seems silly to leave only to come back for that," he answered, even though the truth was that he was using his cousin's wedding as an excuse to buy him those few days with Mara before he had to say goodbye. Which was something he was finding difficult even to think about. Especially after the night they'd just spent together.

"Maybe between Mara and I, we can get you to actually venture out onto the streets of Northbridge again before I go," he added.

"Between you and Mara..." Celeste reiterated. "You like her, don't you?"

It somehow felt like more than that, but he said, "Sure. What's not to like?"

His grandmother smiled weakly. "There's nothing about her not to like. Poor thing must have been more worried about me than she was letting on because when I talked to her on the phone to tell her what had happened with Armand, she broke down and cried."

For reasons Jared couldn't understand that made him ache inside and wish he'd been there with her.

As if his grandmother sensed what he was thinking, Celeste said, "I keep wondering if something might be developing between the two of you."

Jared answered her smile with a shrug. "Something. Maybe," he conceded. "I just don't know what, exactly. Or where it can go from here."

"Why?"

"I'm not good at that kind of thing—relationships. A lot of women have tried to hold my interest but none have succeeded."

"Women like Stephanie. Women who have a lot to offer," Celeste guessed.

"Stephanie was one of them, yes."

"And now here's Mara, a simple, small-town girl. If someone like Stephanie couldn't hold your interest, how could Mara?"

That rubbed him wrong but he wasn't sure why. "Stephanie doesn't have anything over Mara."

Celeste's smile strengthened.

"Besides, there's this town," Jared continued. "Mara is chin-deep in it with no intention of ever leaving it or her family. And that's definitely not for me."

"Why not?"

"You, of all people, should know—there was a time when you were willing to do anything to get out of here."

"And then willing to do anything to get back in," she said with a small laugh.

"Yeah, about that," Jared said. "You were miserable here before. How could you have been happy when you came back—especially living an even more stifled life?"

"I thought that was clear—I was miserable before because of Armand."

"And because of the town," Jared reminded her. "And the terrible pressures on you—I felt them myself growing up—"

"But would what the town expected of a minister's family have been so bad if Armand were different?" Celeste mused. "For me, I don't think it would have been. I think he made things a hundred times worse than they needed to be."

"Okay, granted," Jared said, thinking that that had

the ring of what Mara contended about Jared's opinion of Northbridge; he blamed the town for what was actually the fault of his grandfather and the restrictions and limitations the Reverend had put on him. But that still didn't answer his initial question, so he reworded it and asked it again. "All it took was being in Northbridge as someone not connected to the Reverend for you not to feel penned in here, then?"

"Yes."

"Come on, seriously," he cajoled. "How is that possible?"

Celeste smiled again. "Because here I had you," she said as if it were an obvious answer. "Even from a distance, even though none of you knew it, I've had your dad and Jack and all my grandchildren."

"And that's been enough? Even from a distance?" Jared said, skepticism tingeing his voice.

"I can't say I wouldn't have liked to have had more contact, been closer with you all. But yes, even from a distance, just being able to look in on your lives was better than nothing. That's the biggest thing I learned all those years—that the people you love are what's important. They're everything. And when I didn't have that, I had nothing. I had an empty life. Like I'm afraid you're going to have."

"An empty life?" Jared repeated with a laugh. "Mara thinks I have a bleak future, now you think I have an empty life?"

"Mara thinks you have a bleak future?" Celeste asked.

Rather than answering that, Jared said, "My life is not empty. I have everything."

Celeste only smiled again, and Jared wondered if he was mistaken or if there was some sadness—or even pity—in her smile this time.

Then his grandmother said, "You don't have anyone who fills your life and makes it grow, who gives it value and brings you real joy, who shares it with you, who helps you build it into more than it is."

"Are you going to start talking about cats and old ladies going to auctions to buy antique butter churns, too?"

His grandmother's weathered brow wrinkled in confusion.

"Never mind," he said rather than explain his reference to what Mara had said when they'd discussed his 'bleak future.'

"I don't know about cats or those other things," Celeste said then. "But I do know that you think we're alike, you and I. You think we're alike from before—when I needed to get away and when you did, too. But I see similarities from a different time. I see the way you are now and the way I was when I was gone from Northbridge, too."

"I promise you I'm not on the lam," Jared joked.

"But you don't have anyone, either," Celeste said, ignoring his levity. "You only have your work—the way I only had jobs that occupied some of my hours. Then I would go home to my rented room or apartment, and just pass more hours until I could go back to work. You may have friends or girlfriends you socialize with, but mostly you don't have anyone you care about or who cares about you above all else and in every way. And I'm sad for you."

So she was pitying him.

Jared didn't like it.

But before he could say anything about it, his grandmother went on. "I know I don't know you the way I would if we'd been close all these years, and I'm not a part of the life you've lived since you've left Northbridge. But I've kept up with you every way I could. I've listened to everything the family has had to say about you, I've read about you, seen your picture in newspapers and magazines, and you always seem so intense, so alone. Not happy."

"Just because I'm not married—"

Celeste didn't allow for more of that excuse. She cut him off and continued with what she'd been saying. "I know, too, that you don't think you care much for Northbridge. But now I've had the chance to be with you, to talk with you, to really see you and start to get to know you. And I only feel it more strongly—you *are* alone outside of Northbridge, much like I was when I was traveling, trying to get back."

"Oh, I don't know about that," he scoffed.

His grandmother ignored that, seeming determined to get out all she wanted to say about him. "But while you've been here, when you're with Mara, you seem happier. You *look* happier. So what I'm wondering is, if something *is* developing between you two, maybe you should stop thinking like the boy who needed to escape the way his misguided grandmother did, and start thinking like the grandmother who opened her eyes one day and all of a sudden knew what really mattered."

Chapter Ten

Within minutes of leaving his grandmother's apartment, Jared was parked in front of Mara's house. He'd asked when he'd said goodbye to her that morning if it would be all right to stop by later even if he couldn't tell her exactly when. She'd given him the okay, and the thought that he was going to get to see her again had carried him through all the hours between then and now.

But here he was and all he could do was sit there. He left the engine running so he could have heat as he stared out his windshield, stalled suddenly by the strangest feeling.

He wasn't sure where the feeling had come from. Or what it was. And he wondered if it had anything to do with what Celeste had said to him about her concerns that he had an empty life, if that might have just hit him for some reason. That and the similar prediction Mara had made recently that he was facing a bleak future.

Even though he hadn't thought he'd taken those odd comments too seriously, they *were* rattling around in his brain. Were they affecting him more than he thought?

Possibly. But when he dissected the feeling, it didn't seem to have its deepest roots there.

No, he realized after a moment. What had slammed him the minute he'd pulled up in front of the house was something that had to do only with Mara, with wanting to see her so badly he felt as if he could literally bound out of that car and run to her door.

It was an urge—a driving force—that he could honestly say he'd never felt before. Which was probably why it struck him as so strange.

Yet here he was, almost desperate to get to her. And not merely to get to her. He also had the bizarre desire to tell her every small detail of his day, to rehash it, to discuss it with her. To hear what she'd done since he'd left her. To talk about her getting upset when his grandmother had called to say everything was resolved, to make sure she was all right. To hug her and hold her if she still needed it. To kiss her and then go from there....

But what he was craving wasn't altogether physical—which surprised him, too. Because, while the night before had been incredible, what he wanted as much as a repeat of that was a simple, nonsexual reconnection with her, too. It was as if he couldn't actually put the day and everything that had happened behind him until he went through it with her, until he had her as a sounding board to put everything into perspective, to center him again, to pull him completely out of what the day had brought so it could fade into the background, and he could go on to something better. With her.

Okay, he hadn't had much sleep the previous night because they'd made love through most of it. And yes, it had been a stressful day. But he'd had enough to eat; he hadn't had anything mind-altering to drink. And unless he was mistaken, he hadn't gone nuts. So what *was* this?

He'd never felt compelled to touch base with anyone before. He'd never given a damn if, when he got home, there was anybody there to talk to about how he'd spent his day. And even if there *was* someone there, he rarely ever *did* talk about his day. Or the other person's. In fact, listening to whoever he was with talk about the routine things they'd done was never on his wish list. And he'd sure as hell never felt as if talking to anyone he was personally involved with was what it would take to put everything in the right order again.

But that didn't change the fact that, at that moment, he was itching to go up to that house, ring the doorbell, have Mara open the door and…

Welcome him home? Was that actually what he'd been thinking? That Mara would open the door and he would feel as if he were home?

It *was* what had passed through his mind.

Not that this house felt like home because it didn't. It was just the Pratts' big old house. But to see Mara? To talk to her? Just to be with her? When he imagined it, when he tried it on for size, it did actually give him the sense of coming home.

Wow.

How had that happened? *When* had that happened? *Why* had it happened?

Maybe Celeste's empty-life theory and Mara's bleak-future stuff really had gotten to him more than he'd thought.

Maybe spending most of his time in Northbridge in the company of women had made him soft.

Maybe just being in this damn homey town was costing him his edge.

Maybe he should skip visiting Mara, find Noah, throw back a six-pack, play pool and argue football.

That wasn't what he wanted to do, though. Or what he was going to do. Not with Mara a mere front yard away, waiting for him.

He just didn't understand what was going through him and taking a minute to figure it out seemed wise.

Had the empty-life theory and the bleak-future stuff made more of an impact than he'd realized? he asked himself.

It wasn't easy to buy that. Empty life? Bleak

future? Those were hard sells. He had more money than he knew what to do with. He had houses, apartments, condominiums around the world. He had a penthouse in New York. He even owned an entire section of a Caribbean island. He had cars, boats, his own plane. He had power, prestige. He could go anywhere, do anything, anytime he pleased.

Yes, he'd been antsy lately. Bored. Unchallenged. But he'd attributed that to a lagging interest in his work and that still couldn't be discounted.

But now he wasn't so sure that his work was the only cause of the dissatisfaction he'd been wrestling with.

Was his life empty despite all the perks?

He *had* structured it around work, devoted it to work, filled it with work. Now that that work had become less exciting to him—and now that Celeste and Mara had brought it up—was it registering somewhere in his subconscious that he didn't have anything else to fill the void? Where *did* he see himself down the road? Continuing with work that didn't thrill him anymore?

He *had* conceded to Mara that his life might be lacking a certain dimension. And if that didn't change, he could see where it might lead to a less-than-fulfilling future.

So what was he doing sitting in front of her house feeling the way he was feeling? Was he grabbing on to the first thing that happened into his path to add that other dimension? Latching on to

Mara and finding some sense of coming home to accomplish it?

Just thinking of Mara like that, reducing her to a convenient quick fix, gave him the same reaction he'd had when Celeste had made the reference to Mara being somehow less than Stephanie—it rubbed him wrong. Stephanie *didn't* have anything over Mara, and Mara was so much more than a convenient quick fix.

So much more…

And not just because she had that fresh country-cream beauty and a body that meshed with his as if it had been molded especially for him.

Mara was insightful. Wise. Ambitious. Creative. She was even brave—maybe it was his net worth, or the fact that he could buy and sell entire small countries if he put his mind to it, but no other woman had ever said the kinds of things to him that Mara had and risked pissing him off. People—particularly women—tended to walk on eggshells around him. Cater to him. Concede to him. Agree with him.

But Mara? There hadn't been any tiptoeing around with her. And he liked that. He appreciated it. It made things more interesting. It was freeing because he didn't have to be constantly wondering if his opinions were being supported because of who he was. He didn't have to worry that Mara was only trying to please him or win him over by doing something she might really hate. With Mara, things were straightforward. He could trust that. He could let down his guard with her.

And he *had* let down his guard with her.

And maybe because of that, she'd slipped in somewhere no one else ever had.

That possibility gave him pause.

Had Mara slipped in somehow where no one else ever had? he asked himself. Some place where now, the thought of life without her *did* seem empty? Someplace where, now, the thought of a future without her *did* seem bleak?

The questions answered themselves and, in that instant, light dawned for him.

"The small-town girl's gotcha," he muttered to himself as if he were talking to someone else.

But now that it had sifted in, he knew it was true. She had him. Just the way he sometimes quietly bought off share after share of an ailing company, little by little taking his hold, and then stepping in to the surprise of the owners to let them know they now answered to him, Mara had quietly, subtly, taken him over.

Not that he thought she'd planned or manipulated or maneuvered anything. He knew that wasn't the case. But somehow, when he wasn't looking, he'd come under her control.

"She owns you," he said aloud again, laughing slightly at himself.

But the more he thought about it and realized that it was true, the easier he found it to accept. He was okay with it, he decided. He was okay with the idea of Mara being so important to him—so vital to him—that life without her, a future without her, seemed empty and bleak.

What might not be so okay, though, he thought as he considered the changes that new ownership could mean, was the fact that she was so enmeshed in Northbridge. And Northbridge was the one place he'd never wanted to come back to, not even for a visit, let alone to live.

But even as that went through his head he recalled another point both Mara and Celeste had made—that he blamed the town for what were really acts of his grandfather.

Were they right about that, too?

That was tougher to concede. Northbridge was still a small town with small-town limitations. It was still the place where he'd felt trapped. The place he'd needed to get away from. He wasn't so sure about reconnecting with *that*.

The people not the place—that had been Celeste's lesson learned. Could it work for him as well? he asked himself.

He honestly didn't know. But he hoped so. Because while he wasn't ecstatic about the idea of having an even greater tie to the small town than he already had, or of being anywhere near his grandfather again, he knew he had to have Mara. And if having Mara meant taking Northbridge into the bargain, he was willing to give it a try.

He just hoped Northbridge didn't end up feeling as stifling and stagnant as it had before.

Because in spite of how or when or why it had happened, he knew now that Mara had become the one thing—the one person—he not only wanted, but the one element, the dimension, that he *needed* in order to keep his life from being empty, his future from being bleak.

And he was going to do whatever it took to have her.

After a night with almost no sleep, and a worry-filled day that had culminated in a call from Celeste to let her know the Reverend had exonerated the older women, Mara was drained. Had Jared not asked if he could stop by sometime tonight, she would have gone to bed after her conversation with Celeste.

And yet it only took opening her front door at nearly eleven o'clock Sunday night and seeing Jared standing on her porch to make something flood through her that was warm and sparkling and made her feel energized all over again.

"I wasn't sure you were going to make it here tonight," she greeted him, gorging on the sight of him—tall, handsome, his face showing a sexy shadow of beard that let her know he'd come straight to her from a long day with his family and their trials and tribulations.

He was dressed in that dashing coat over English tweed slacks and a turtleneck sweater that again made him look far too continental for Northbridge. And Mara just wanted to leap into his arms, feel them wrap around her, have his big body envelop hers and forget everything else.

But she'd spent the day reminding herself that the previous evening's romp could only be a one-night stand. She'd known going in that no kind of long-term relationship could come of it, and just because she'd be seeing him again didn't change that. So she tried to maintain some poise and stepped back to let him in.

"I'm sorry it's so late," he apologized as he took off his coat and hung it on the hall tree while she closed the door. "To be honest, I've been here a while. Sitting outside in the car."

"You have?" Mara asked, confused. "Were you waiting to see if I had psychic powers and would guess that you were out there?"

He gave her a small, serene smile and shook his head. "I was thinking about you."

That didn't clear things up.

"Okay," Mara said, wondering if there had been celebrating after the Reverend's statement and Jared had been drinking, even though he didn't seem drunk and he smelled only of that great cologne.

He didn't wait for her to ask him into the living room but just headed there with her in tow. Then he sat on the sofa's center cushion and patted the spot beside him.

Mara joined him on the couch but only tentatively. Primly almost, not sitting too close.

She'd never had a one-night stand before and

wasn't sure how things were supposed to go at the next meeting. Of course, she also wasn't sure what she'd do if he wanted a two-night stand—or even a three- or a four-night stand. She'd lectured herself sternly throughout the day about not just being his fling. But making love with him had been so fantastic she wasn't sure she wouldn't settle for nothing more than a brief interlude if it meant a few more nights with him. If only she could keep in mind that that still wouldn't translate into anything permanent.

"How are you?" Jared asked then.

He angled himself to face her. One elbow was on top of the sofa back and despite the slight distance she'd left between them he didn't hesitate to reach over and curve his hand around her nape. He brushed feathery strokes of his thumb into the hair she'd left falling free when she'd done herself up in her best butt-hugging jeans and a formfitting camisole under a V-neck T-shirt.

"I'm good," she said.

He'd sounded as if he were worried that something was wrong with her and that confused her as much as his sitting outside thinking about her rather than coming in as soon as he'd arrived. Again she wondered if he'd been drinking, but she still saw no signs of it.

"Celeste said you broke down on the phone," he said then, explaining his concern at last.

"Oh," she said, a little embarrassed but also secretly pleased to know he cared. "It was just such a relief to know that it's finally all over with. How's Celeste doing? She said she was glad to have an end to the whole thing, but she sounded kind of shaky herself."

"Did she tell you she passed out cold?"

"No," Mara said with surprise and concern of her own. "At the hospital? Is she all right?"

Jared nodded. "Apparently relief hit her hard, too. But she's okay now. I got her back to the apartment, we had dinner, I gave her a couple of shots of brandy and she was ready to turn in for the night when I left. She said to tell you she'd see you tomorrow."

"Is she planning to come in to work?" Mara asked hopefully.

"She didn't say that. She wouldn't even commit when I said maybe you and I could get her to leave the apartment this week."

"You and I—" Mara repeated. "Are you going to be here this week?" She was feeling her way along and hanging more hopes on what he'd said than she knew she should. But suddenly the idea of the two-night or three-night or four-night stand seemed worth what she might suffer when he did leave town again—if only she could have those nights.

"I told Celeste that I'd stay until after the wedding next Saturday, but now I might be staying longer than that," he said with a slow, sly smile.

Uh-oh, that could be dangerous. She wasn't sure she could keep her feelings under control if she spent a short time with him. If it drew out, she knew she wouldn't be able to.

"You might be staying longer?" she asked, unable to keep a hint of trepidation from her tone.

Jared laughed. "I thought maybe that would be good news but it doesn't sound like it is."

Mara didn't respond. Then she said, "You don't have to get back to work?"

"It isn't as if I have a boss telling me I have to. And I realized tonight that some changes need to be made—maybe from a career standpoint, but definitely from a personal one. That's what I was sitting in the car thinking about."

"I thought you were thinking about me?"

"They seem to go hand in hand."

She wished he'd stop massaging her neck. It felt wonderful and made concentrating on what he was saying complicated.

"What kind of changes?" she managed to ask.

"It's no wonder you and Celeste are so close, you think alike," he said rather than answering *her* question this time. "She and I had a talk tonight, and where you're convinced I'm facing a bleak future, she's worried that I'm living an empty life right now."

"Those sound like two different things," Mara pointed out, shifting so she could face him completely but at the same time moving enough so that he had to stop rubbing her neck. Which he did, laying his hand along the back cushion as his so-pale-blue eyes looked into hers.

"My grandmother thinks my current life is empty

because all I have is work, and you think my future is bleak for the same reason," he explained.

"Ah."

"And you know what?"

Mara raised her eyebrows in question.

"I just, in the last hour, realized that you're both right. With some qualification."

He seemed so calm, so happy to have come to whatever conclusion he'd come to. Mara wished she felt the same way, but for no tangible reason, she was getting increasingly tense.

"What's the qualification?" she asked hesitantly.

"You are."

That didn't make sense either.

"Did you have a few shots of brandy, too?" she asked.

He laughed. "No, I didn't. Why? Do you think I'm drunk?"

Mara shrugged. "How am I the qualification?"

"Something's gone wrong with work—it's not doing it for me anymore, but I don't think that's just because it's all I have going on."

"It was just a thought I was throwing out at you," she reminded.

"And you made a point that seems to be gaining strength the more I mull it over," he said, surprising her. "But I don't think work is just becoming not enough for me. I think there's more wrong on that front. But I realized tonight that there *is* something to the bleak-future, empty-life stuff in a way that doesn't have anything to do with my career."

He went on to tell her how he'd felt when he'd first parked out front, how he hadn't been sure exactly what it was that he'd been feeling, and the conclusions he'd reached when he'd broken the feelings down to their core.

"It's all about you," he concluded. "And now that there *is* you, life *without* you does seem as if it would be empty. And a future *without* you? Bleak for sure."

Mara didn't know what to say.

Jared didn't seem to notice that she was dumbstruck.

"So," he said, "I thought maybe we'd see if we might be able to work this out."

"To work what—exactly—out?" she asked, as if through a fog.

"This—you and me."

"I didn't know there was a you and me," Mara said quietly.

"Last night was pretty you-and-me, wasn't it?"

"Last night was pretty you-and-me, yes," she hedged, not committing too much to something she'd believed to be a one-night stand.

He frowned. "But you're not up for more than that?" he asked.

He'd never know just how *up* for it she could have been. And as she looked at him, at the face that stole her breath, at the body her own wanted more than it wanted food or water, it would have been so easy to push aside what she knew about him, what she knew about herself, and just jump in with both feet.

But she couldn't push aside what she knew about him or what she knew about herself. Not if they were talking about more than a brief interlude.

"It isn't that I'm not *up* for it," she said. "I just don't think it would…work."

"Why not?"

"I think it's just what feels right to you for the moment. What's absorbed all your time and thought and energy has lost its zing for you, and now here you are, and I'm sort of a novelty, a distraction. Maybe you're touching base with what feels familiar and comfortable, and so that seems like a direction you should take. But—"

"A quick fix," he named it. "I thought about that and that's not it," he insisted.

"But," she continued, "I don't believe it could last for you."

"You're worried that I couldn't be happy in Northbridge," he guessed. "And I can't swear that I will be, but I think Celeste may have made a good point, that the place doesn't matter as much as the person you're with. And you're the person I want to be with."

"It's not only Northbridge—it's much more than that—but that's something to think about, too."

"If it isn't only Northbridge, then what is it?"

"It's—it's you and I. You're a person who sees what you want and pulls out all the stops to get it. But you aren't the 'follow-through guy'—as Stephanie said. Once you take control of a company, you send in other people to do the cleanup and you move on. That's a lot like what my father did, what Derek did—they weren't follow-through guys either. They saw what they wanted, they went after it and once they had it, they moved on, and it was other people who had to take care of what they left behind. My mom was the cleanup person with my father. I was the cleanup person with Derek. I can't—I won't— be the cleanup person ever again. Even if that is what I do for a living, I won't do it again in the rest of my life."

"I'm absolutely *not* agreeing with that, but what do you see me leaving behind for you to clean up? I don't have a sick father *or* seven kids."

"But there could be kids down the road—I *want* kids and—"

"I wouldn't leave my family," he said, sounding slightly angry that she would even suggest it.

"You're not a person who sticks around, Jared," Mara insisted in spite of his being miffed. "Especially not around here."

"I'm coming to see what both you and Celeste said about Northbridge, too," he said. "I *have* blamed the town for what really came from the Reverend—"

"But it's still a small town and you haven't exactly embraced the good side of that while you've been here."

"It's you I want, Mara. If that has to be here, then

I can live with that. I've seen that there is a good side and that Northbridge isn't what I thought it was, growing up. Who knows, I may learn to love it the way you do."

"And if you don't? If you discover that you hate it as much as you did before? That it suffocates you just the same?"

"We'll build an oxygen chamber," he said facetiously. "Northbridge isn't an issue."

"Maybe it isn't the biggest issue, but it's an issue."

"And the biggest issue is that you don't believe I can make a commitment to you and stick with it."

"I want to," she confessed in a voice that was so small it was almost a whisper. "I want to more than I can tell you. But—"

"No buts."

"Yes buts," she said more firmly. "I can't do it, Jared. I want a future I can count on. That doesn't mean wondering every day if it's going to come to an end because, like my father and Derek—even like Celeste once upon a time—you get bored and need more excitement or bigger frontiers to conquer the way you did when you left at eighteen."

"I was a kid and I needed to get out on my own, grow up. I needed to get away from the vise grip the Reverend kept trying to have on me. That isn't the same as running out on a family and running out on a family isn't something I would do," he said seriously.

Mara felt awful accusing him of that sort of character flaw when it might be unfounded, but it didn't alter her sense that it was possible. And if it was possible, she couldn't open the door to it. Or to him.

"Maybe you *wouldn't* run out on a family and I'm misjudging you, and if that's true, I'm sorry. But when I look at how you handle businesses or corporations after you take them over, it seems like a warning. When I look at things like Stephanie saying your heart wasn't in your relationship with her, and the fact that you agreed yourself that that was true of all your relationships with women—"

"It was true of them all before. Not now. Now my heart's so damn far in you're killing me with this."

He did look hurt and offended and angry and full of disbelief at what she was saying, and Mara hated that she was causing it all. But she could only shake her head and go on.

"—and when I look at how you've still turned a cold shoulder to the place I make my home and never want to leave, on top of everything else, I just don't think there's hope for things working out."

And if she was going to lose him sooner or later— which she was too afraid was a foregone conclusion— she'd rather lose him now, when it was her own choice, and before she got in any deeper with him. Before being left might mean being left holding the bag.

Before it meant being hurt—worse than she was hurting right at this moment....

"So it just can't happen," she told him.

"It could happen if we made it happen," he contended.

She shook her head. "I won't take the chance."

"That's really what it boils down to, isn't it? You look at me and see a gamble, the kind your mother took with your father, the kind you took with Derek, the kind you both lost on, and so you won't take the chance on me."

"I guess that *is* what it boils down to," she admitted quietly.

He shook his head this time. "If Celeste hadn't risked coming back here she wouldn't have had the one thing she wanted most after making the biggest mistake of her life. She wouldn't have been able to at least be near my dad and my uncle and her grandchildren. She took the chance because we were that important to her. Because we were what mattered to her. I'm willing to take the chance on this town again because *you're* what's important to me. Because *you* are what matters to me."

He took her hand between both of his, holding it gently in the warmth she remembered all too vividly coursing over every inch of her naked body the previous night.

"Gamble one more time, Mara," he tempted then. "I promise you, you're the first in a long line of what I will follow through on."

But if he didn't, how horrible that would be!

That was all she could think about.

Unbearably horrible.

Worse—so much worse—than when Derek had left her. As bad as when her father had left her mother and Celeste had been the only salvation for the seven Pratt kids and the woman who had barely survived the heartbreak to raise them…

Mara swallowed an enormous lump in her throat and shook her head yet again. "No," she said firmly.

She pulled her hand from between his, aware of how exposed it felt to lose the comfort of that cocoon, how wrong it somehow seemed.

"You can let yourself out," she told him in a voice so soft it was a scant utterance. But it was the best she could do as she stood and made a fast escape up the stairs because it seemed totally insane to reject him and deny herself what she suddenly wanted more than she'd allowed herself to consider, and then break down as if he'd rejected her.

But breaking down was exactly what she did, barely making it behind the closed door of her bedroom before she sank onto the end of the bed where they'd made such mind-altering love Saturday night, sobbing as the sound of Jared going out the front door put a final ending to everything between them.

Chapter Eleven

The wedding of Mara's brother Cam and Jared's cousin Eden was the following Saturday at four o'clock in the afternoon. Since her Sunday-night breakup with Jared, Mara had been dreading it. She'd done everything she could to avoid running into him all week, but the wedding itself was the one time that was impossible.

The only positive aspect of it, she'd told herself as she donned her short, slinky, spaghetti-strapped black dress and three-inch-high heels in preparation for the event, was that once the wedding was over, Jared would surely be leaving Northbridge and she wouldn't have to spend every minute of every day worrying about seeing him around every corner.

And yet, as she sat alone on one side of the church's basement where the reception was being held, that same thought somehow depressed her even more—Jared would surely be leaving Northbridge now…

Not that the emotional seesaw hadn't been happening the entire week: She wanted him. She couldn't let herself have him.

Maybe things could work out.

Maybe it would be disastrous for her if they *did* get together.

Maybe he *would* learn to love Northbridge.

Maybe he never would and that would be his excuse to leave *her* with seven kids.

But she wanted him.

She just couldn't let herself have him….

And so it had gone. Day in, day out, since last Sunday night.

It had been a very, very long; dreary; awful week.

And now here she was, unable even to taste the luscious cake in front of her and equally as unable to stop looking at Jared at the opposite end of the room.

She just wanted him so much.

Would that go away—or at least get better—when he'd left town? Because it didn't seem as if it would. The man was on her mind constantly. He was in her dreams. And it wasn't only thinking about him, or wondering what he was doing or where he was, or picturing him in her mind's eye. She had a yearning to be with him that was so intense it was nearly driving her crazy.

She'd never been such a mess, not even when Derek had divorced her.

And she was worried that it *wasn't* going to get better when Jared left town.

Or ever…

He looked outrageously handsome and that didn't help anything. He was wearing a suit that fitted like a song written especially for him. It was dark blue and cast just a hint more color into his pale eyes.

At least she thought it did. She could have been imagining that because, after all, she hadn't seen him close-up.

How could she have when he hadn't come anywhere near her?

Was he merely being considerate and giving her some space? she wondered. Or was she giving off stay-away vibes?

Or maybe he just didn't want contact with her.

As much as she knew that they *shouldn't* have contact, she couldn't help wishing that he might come over and at least say hello.

But he didn't. He hadn't. Not through the half hour before the ceremony when everyone had mingled in the church lobby. Not after the short, simple ceremony as everyone had sifted downstairs and through the receiving line. Not during the last two hours of dining and dancing and chatting when he appeared to have talked to everyone else there. He'd stayed away from Mara. And while it wasn't as if he was having a raucous good time, he did seem to be having a better time than she was.

He also appeared to be calmer than she felt, she thought. More relaxed. More comfortable with the situation, maybe even with the outcome of last Sunday night.

Easy come, easy go? Was that what she'd been for him? Because she didn't think he could be suffering what she was suffering and be so cool about it.

He'd been talking for a few minutes with a city councilman while Mara continued to watch him, and when the man walked off, Celeste joined Jared.

Celeste slipped a casual arm around his waist with a familiarity that had apparently grown this last week when they'd been together without Mara.

After a lot of talking and persuading on Mara's part, Celeste had been convinced to come to the wedding. It was the older woman's first foray into public in Northbridge since her identity had been revealed and Mara thought it was going well. The Reverend had been released from the hospital but had opted against attending the event, so there wasn't the pall he brought with him wherever he went. Instead, Celeste's maiden voyage into society again and her first venture into a Perry celebration as a member of the family was only upbeat. She'd been welcomed by her sons, daughters-in-law and the rest of her grandchildren, and by the lion's share of friends and acquaintances, too.

As Mara looked on, Jared smiled down at his

grandmother. He laughed at something the older woman said. He put an arm around her, too. And Celeste beamed.

Mara hadn't found much to smile about since Sunday night but seeing that brought one on. She was thrilled for her old friend. She could see by the cherry-redness of Celeste's cheeks and the pure joy that emanated from the older woman that she wasn't sorry to have come, and Mara was glad that finally— after decades of doing all she could simply to be in some proximity to her family—Celeste could now be a genuine part of it. If anyone deserved it, Mara thought, it was Celeste.

But that still didn't lessen how difficult it was for Mara to view it only from far away. To witness the good time they were having when she wanted badly to be with them both, to be included.

But there she was, on the outside looking in, the way Celeste had spent so many years.

How had Celeste stood it? she wondered.

She knew, though, that for her friend, it hadn't been a case of enduring something painful. It had been a blessing just to be near the people Celeste loved.

And it had been the only choice Celeste had had. Which wasn't true of Mara. She knew she could get up from that table right then, cross that room and tell Jared she'd changed her mind. That she would gamble on him.

But what if she did that and lost?

It just kept coming back to that and that's what glued her to her seat.

No more gambles.

Although on the heels of that thought she recalled that she had never considered Derek a gamble in any way. She'd grown up with him. She'd been certain she knew him. It hadn't seemed like even a remote possibility that she was taking a risk with him. But obviously she had been.

At least this time she'd seen it coming so she'd had the opportunity to keep from taking the risk, she told herself.

And what it was costing her was not being over there with Jared. Not being with someone she cared about so much it made her ache all over.

So she was already losing, she thought.

Maybe it was only because she felt so bad, but she began to wonder if that really was the way to go— losing rather than even taking a chance on winning.

Where would Celeste have been if she hadn't run the risk that day, years ago, and ventured back into Northbridge to see if anyone recognized her? She would have been left with nothing.

Which is what I have now…

But Celeste had taken a calculated risk and it had paid off—maybe not well enough to have allowed her to be involved with her family, but it had paid off to the extent that she'd been able to bear witness from afar as her sons had grown and blossomed, had matured and had families of their own.

So maybe I should calculate the risk...

Or maybe she was just grasping at straws.

But still she began to reconsider the reasons she'd sent Jared packing.

They were all valid reasons, she realized. He *was* the person who put things into motion and then, once he had his stronghold, handed off the rest to his delegates while he started to put something else into motion somewhere else.

But was it a character flaw? Did it say something damning about his entire nature?

Possibly. But even though he'd moved out of Northbridge, out of Montana, he hadn't turned his back on his family. He'd kept in touch, in close contact with everyone but his grandfather—there was follow-through with that.

And when he'd learned who Celeste was, he'd rushed back here for her, he'd championed her, he'd done everything he could to help the grandmother he hadn't even known. He'd put effort into *getting* to know her, into establishing a relationship when he could have simply ignored her.

Those were good things. Signs of commitments he kept, ties he didn't sever. The kinds of commitments and ties that her father, that Derek, *had* severed. The kind of a tie she might become. Certainly the kind his own kids would be if he had any.

So maybe what was true of him in his work might not be so true of him personally, even if no woman had yet formed one of those ties to prove or disprove it.

Okay, not conclusive, but not altogether negative, either, Mara decided.

What about the worry that she was nothing more than a distraction from the slump he'd found himself in lately?

Also still a possibility. Although, wouldn't Celeste and returning to Northbridge and simply getting away have been enough? He hadn't needed to pursue her to take his mind off his suddenly unsatisfying career.

But he *had* pursued her. He *had* seemed to enjoy her company, to want to prolong it. He *had* kept coming back for more. And if she was nothing but a novelty? Would she have been able to hold his interest at all, let alone bring him to where he'd been Sunday night when he'd tried so hard to work things out with her?

She wasn't sure. But that, too, seemed possible.

And then there was Northbridge itself.

Jared *hadn't* discovered that he loved the small town. And even though he was hanging onto Celeste's theory that it was the people—not the place—that mattered, would it be true for him the way it had been for his grandmother? And what if it wasn't?

Would I leave to be with him? Mara asked herself.

Not eagerly. But she was stunned to discover that the idea didn't send her running for cover. Instead, it was something she didn't want to entertain, but thought she might be able to if she had to. Because one thing she realized as she considered staying in

Northbridge without Jared was that it seemed suddenly to hold less appeal.

She liked being with him, talking to him—more than anyone she'd ever encountered in the small town she loved so much. He made her laugh. He made her think outside the box and stretch mental muscles she didn't ordinarily need to stretch in her everyday life. She liked the parts of him that *weren't* the hometown boy anymore, and staying in Northbridge without him to make it seem somehow brighter and sharper and more interesting might change it for her now.

But would she be happy somewhere else just because she was with him?

She didn't know.

Which made it yet another gamble.

It was all dicey, she decided. There were no carved-in-stone answers and regardless of how hard she tried, she couldn't convince herself beyond the shadow of a doubt that things would work out between them.

But maybe, she thought, nothing was without risk whether she saw the risk ahead of time—like with Jared—or she didn't—like with Derek.

Or at least, maybe nothing worth having was without risk.

And Jared? She couldn't think of anything more worth having than Jared.

Before she'd even realized she was going to do it, Mara was out of her chair, crossing the church basement, headed in his direction.

The music went on playing, the dancers on the dance floor went on dancing, none of the conversations dwindled, and yet to Mara everything felt as if it had stopped as her senses, her thoughts, her attention centered on Jared and only on Jared.

She wanted him—in a sea of uncertainty that was the sole undeniable fact. In spite of any risk. In spite of how big the gamble might be.

It wasn't until she reached him that it struck her that she didn't know how to put that into words.

"I'll leave you two alone," Celeste muttered instantly.

Mara knew only at that moment that the older woman—who hadn't said a single word to her all week about Jared—had not been silent because she hadn't known there was anything going on. Celeste had apparently just thought to stay out of their business. But right then Mara could have used a little moral support, and instead she found herself standing face-to-face with the man himself, his clear-as-glass eyes on her alone as she looked up at him and drew a complete blank when it came to what to say.

"Hi," he said quietly, filling the single word with the kind of intimacy that had been in his voice last Sunday morning in bed.

"I feel like I'm about to buy a lottery ticket with the last dollar to my name," she blurted out as if that would make any sense to him.

But it actually seemed to, because, as if he knew

precisely what was on her mind, he said, "Let me see if I can't make it a little less scary than that."

He took that fantastic coat of his from the back of a chair and wrapped it around her bare arms and shoulders, then he clasped her hand in his and, without another word, he led her out into the early darkness.

He went directly to his rental car in the parking lot, opened the passenger door, and waited for her to get in.

"We're going somewhere?" she asked.

He merely smiled and waited.

Maybe they were going to talk in the car, Mara thought, getting in.

When she had, he closed the door and rounded the car to slide behind the wheel.

Still without giving her any information, he started the engine and pulled out of the church lot.

"Where—?"

"You'll see. Give me a minute."

Mara told herself that if they were going to drive in silence she should organize her thoughts so she could say something coherent. But she was too curious to accomplish that and instead tried to figure out what was going on.

They were about a quarter of a mile outside of Northbridge proper when he turned off the main road onto a private drive that had been festooned for a long while with a For Sale sign that was no longer in sight.

"This is the old McQuire place. The McQuire kids have been trying to unload it since their folks passed away," Mara said.

Jared only smiled again—a closed-lipped, Mona Lisa sort of smile.

He drove up the pitted road to the tiny, dilapidated farm house that hadn't seen paint in so many years it was nothing but gray, rotting wood that gave no hint as to what color it might have been once upon a time. Pulling right up to the house itself, Jared stopped the car and turned off the engine. Then he got out, came around to her side again and opened her door, holding out a hand for her to take.

Mara looked from him to the house and back at him, but there were no answers anywhere to be seen. So she accepted his hand because she wanted the feel of it around hers again and kept his coat clamped at her chest to bring it with her as she stepped onto the barren soil that was now the place's front yard.

Jared didn't hesitate to close the car door behind her and lead her up the four cement steps, which were crumbling at the edges, across the splintered wooden porch and into the house.

She knew from having been there in the past that the front door opened into the living room and although Mara couldn't see in the dark, the warmth of heated air greeted them, surprising her, since, to her knowledge, all utilities had been long ago turned off.

Then Jared flipped a switch and lights came on, too.

The house had been cleaned—it was spotless—but it was in no better shape inside than out. The woodwork was chipped or broken, bricks were missing from the fireplace, paint and wallpaper were peeling from the walls, and the hardwood floors were dull and scratched.

"Still kind of scary," Mara said, referring to the only thing Jared had really said to her since she'd joined him at the church.

"I bought it," he announced.

"This house?" Mara asked with a full measure of disbelief.

"The whole property—the house and the fifty acres that go with it."

"You did?"

"Closed the deal this morning."

"What are you going to do with it?"

"Live here."

Mara went from staring at her surroundings to staring at him. "You're going to live *here?*"

"Not in this particular house. It's going to be the construction office for the contractor and the crew who will build a house that's a little better than this one. Then this one will be leveled."

"They'll build a house for you? In Northbridge?" she said as if he had to be kidding.

Jared stepped directly in front of her and grabbed the lapels of his coat in both hands, using it to keep her captive as he smiled down at her.

"I did some thinking this week. Some digging.

Some research. Some looking around. Some soul-searching. And I made two pretty big decisions and the changes to go with them."

"What decisions and changes?"

"First of all, I became one with Northbridge to see if I could stand it."

"That doesn't have a positive ring to it."

"It should, because it turned out more in the pro column than in the con. You—and Celeste—were right to think that what I disliked so much about being here was more about the Reverend—and the way he'd affected my life when I lived here—than about the town itself. And when I did the footwork, got reacquainted with a lot of the people, checked everything out and weighed whether I could live here—"

"When you became *one* with Northbridge," Mara said, gently teasing him about his Zen-like terminology.

"When I became one with Northbridge, I decided I wouldn't have a problem making this my home again."

"Funny, because I just decided that if I had to leave here to be with you, I would," Mara said softly.

Jared's eyebrows reached for his hairline. "Seriously?"

Mara nodded.

"Wow. That's something. You love it here. Your family is here. Your business. Celeste..."

Mara shrugged.

"Well, that makes what *I* was going to suggest as a compromise a lot easier."

"What were you going to suggest?" Mara asked.

"Making our home here but taking a lot of long vacations to keep the blood pumping—New York, the Bahamas, Tahiti, L.A., Europe—"

"I think I could deal with that," Mara said with a laugh at the notion that it might be difficult to persuade her to take vacations anyone would envy.

"Then I think I can deal with making Northbridge my primary residence again," Jared concluded.

"But you bought this awful house and fifty acres the McQuires haven't been able to unload because they overpriced it, *before* making the vacation suggestion?"

"I bought it because I had every intention of moving back here to prove to you that I would—and could—be happy in Northbridge. Plus I was going to need a place of my own to live in while I went on chasing you until you gave in."

"You were in takeover mode," she guessed.

"And you're the target," he confirmed.

"I guess I just made that easy for you," she joked.

"I'm hoping so, but maybe you can tell me a thing or two about what's been going through your head this week."

"Nothing good," she confessed, knowing the time had come for her to give a little. "I haven't been in such terrific spirits and tonight... Tonight I just couldn't fight it anymore. I wanted to be with you, and even though I know there's some risk I also know that's true of everything worthwhile and—"

"And you were even ready to risk leaving Northbridge?"

"Don't look so smug."

"This is not smug, this is glee," he said smugly.

But Mara couldn't have cared less because all that mattered was that she was with him and they were each willing to effect changes to make this work.

"What other decision or change did you make this week?" she asked then.

"I'm revamping my career."

"If you say you've decided to become a kindergarten teacher I'll know you've just gone crazy and you're going to have to be locked up."

He laughed. "No, I'm not going to be a kindergarten teacher. But I did take some of the other things you said to me into consideration, and I realized that Northbridge wasn't all you were right about."

"I'm just brilliant," she said with some mock smugness of her own.

"Insightful—that's what I thought about you."

Mara laughed with some embarrassment because, while she'd been kidding, he hadn't been.

"What words of wisdom did I impart that changed your career path?" she asked then.

"The stuff that pissed me off the most," he said with another laugh. "The stuff about how I've done what the Reverend did in my own work—gone in with all the answers, forced them on the companies I've taken over, made sure everyone bent to my will—"

"Maybe I *don't* want you," Mara joked.

"You'll want the new me," he said with confidence and a sexy cockiness that started her blood pulsating in her veins.

"What's the new you?"

"I'm only using my powers for good, not for evil," he said like a comic-book hero. Then, in his normal voice, he added, "No more takeovers—hostile or otherwise. I'm becoming a consultant instead. I'll offer my services and those of my staff to corporations on the brink of being taken over. We can analyze what's gone wrong and where and how things can be turned around, how a takeover can be avoided. Basically, I'll let them in on what I would do if I were to swallow them up. I decided to be about building—or rebuilding—rather than about breaking things down, building businesses back up to where they can survive, building a house here, building a new life and family with you."

"And all I had to decide was to take a chance," Mara said softly, moved by the revelations he'd had in the same time frame.

"So long as that's the decision you've made, I'm a happy man."

There was a note of question in his tone and as Mara looked into that face she wanted to wake up to every day for the rest of her life, she suddenly had no problem telling him how and why she'd come to the conclusions she had and that she was definitely willing to take the chance on him.

He was smiling again when she finished, calmly, warmly and with satisfaction. "That saves me a lot of trouble. But don't get me wrong—I was willing to go to any lengths to make you see that my heart really is in this with you. My whole heart and soul and mind and body. I'm in love with you, Mara. And that isn't something I've ever felt about—or said to—anyone else."

"I love you, too," she said in a faint voice clogged with emotion.

Jared used the coat lapels to pull her even closer, coming forward himself to kiss her.

Mara snaked her arms from inside the coat to find a way around his waist as she gave in wholly and completely to that kiss, to him.

His lips parted over hers then, deepening the kiss with a curious tongue that came to explore and play.

And as if they'd been apart for far too long, passion was ignited, instantly hot and demanding.

"Here?" Mara said moments later when kissing had gone from hello to *take me now*, when hands had already begun to travel and Jared's jacket and tie had landed in a heap several feet away.

"Why not? We own it," he countered.

"What if we cave in through the floorboards?" she joked.

"Then we'll die happy," he said, whisking his

coat from around her shoulders to spread it on the floor like a blanket.

He kicked off his shoes, flung away his socks and sat in the center of the overcoat at her feet. Then he ran one hand up the inside of Mara's leg to entice her to join him.

She actually didn't have a choice because the feel of that big hand under her skirt turned her knees to jelly and she had to sit with him on the coat lining or collapse. And sitting with him would be so much better.

Clothes flew then as each undressed the other until nothing stood in their way and they made love with wild abandon that reached a climax so intense, so exquisite for Mara she almost couldn't bear it and still wished it would go on and never end.

But even when it did she had the comfort of knowing that it was only the beginning for them, the beginning of so much more.

When they were both totally spent Jared rolled to his back and took her with him to lie molded to his side. Then he pulled the coat around them both as much as he could manage, making sure Mara got the lion's share of the coverage.

"I might need to have this thing bronzed," Mara said in a raspy voice as she settled into the comfort of man and cashmere.

"Which *thing* would that be? Because I might have a complaint to register if you want to bronze—"

"This coat," she clarified with a weary, sated laugh.

"Should I understand that?"

"No," she said, smiling into the warm strength of his shoulder. "Just don't ever throw it away."

"I'll leave discarding things to you. From this point forward I'm into holding on," he said, tightening his arms around her.

Mara kissed his chest. "I love you," she whispered.

"I love you," he whispered back, his mouth pressed to her hair. "I love you in a way that I didn't know was possible to love anyone. It's like you're inside of me. A part of me. The best part of me."

"Don't make me cry," Mara chastised with tears in her voice.

"Never. Not ever," he vowed. "I'm only going to make you cry out the way you did a few minutes ago," he added, lightening the tone again.

One of Mara's legs was over his and she brought the knee that was lounging between his thighs upward until he groaned.

"But not quite yet," he said then. "I don't think I've slept ten hours the whole week, I need a little nap first."

"Already not making good on your promises," Mara said, pretending disappointment when she'd only been tormenting him in the first place. She was too blissfully happy just the way she was to want anything disturbed.

"We have the rest of our lives, you know," he reminded.

"I do know," she said.

And she honestly did. She knew in that moment that her gamble would pay off with the rest of their lives spent together. Suddenly she could feel it in the depths of her soul.

Because no matter what had happened in the past to each of them separately, no matter how they might have failed or what might have been lacking, together they were something greater than either of them had been before.

Something too great to ever come apart.

And regardless of where they ever were, the important thing really was just that they had each other.

* * * * *

Don't miss Victoria Pade's contribution to
Special Edition's in-line continuity
MONTANA MAVERICKS: STRIKING IT RICH,
when A FAMILY FOR THE HOLIDAYS
hits shelves in November 2007!

For a sneak preview of Marie Ferrarella's
DOCTOR IN THE HOUSE,
coming to NEXT in September,
please turn the page.

He didn't look like an unholy terror.

But maybe that reputation was exaggerated, Bailey DelMonico thought as she turned in her chair to look toward the doorway.

The man didn't seem scary at all.

Dr. Munro, or Ivan the Terrible, was tall, with an athletic build and wide shoulders. The cheekbones beneath what she estimated to be day-old stubble were prominent. His hair was light brown and just this side of unruly. Munro's hair looked as if he used his fingers for a comb and didn't care who knew it.

The eyes were brown, almost black as they were aimed at her. There was no other word for it. Aimed.

As if he was debating whether or not to fire at point-blank range.

Somewhere in the back of her mind, a line from a B movie, "Be afraid—be very afraid…" whispered along the perimeter of her brain. Warning her. Almost against her will, it caused her to brace her shoulders. Bailey had to remind herself to breathe in and out like a normal person.

The chief of staff, Dr. Bennett, had tried his level best to put her at ease and had almost succeeded. But an air of tension had entered with Munro. She wondered if Dr. Bennett was bracing himself as well, bracing for some kind of disaster or explosion.

"Ah, here he is now," Harold Bennett announced needlessly. The smile on his lips was slightly forced, and the look in his gray, kindly eyes held a warning as he looked at his chief neurosurgeon. "We were just talking about you, Dr. Munro."

"Can't imagine why," Ivan replied dryly.

Harold cleared his throat, as if that would cover the less than friendly tone of voice Ivan had just displayed. "Dr. Munro, this is the young woman I was telling you about yesterday."

Now his eyes dissected her. Bailey felt as if she was undergoing a scalpel-less autopsy right then and there. "Ah yes, the Stanford Special."

He made her sound like something that was listed at the top of a third-rate diner menu. There was enough contempt in his voice to offend an entire delegation from the UN.

Summoning the bravado that her parents always claimed had been infused in her since the moment she first drew breath, Bailey put out her hand. "Hello. I'm Dr. Bailey DelMonico."

Ivan made no effort to take the hand offered to him. Instead, he slid his long, lanky form bonelessly into the chair beside her. He proceeded to move the chair ever so slightly so that there was even more space between them. Ivan faced the chief of staff, but the words he spoke were addressed to her.

"You're a doctor, DelMonico, when I say you're a doctor," he informed her coldly, sparing her only one frosty glance to punctuate the end of his statement.

Harold stifled a sigh. "Dr. Munro is going to take over your education. Dr. Munro—" he fixed Ivan with a steely gaze that had been known to send lesser doctors running for their antacids, but, as always, seemed to have no effect on the chief neurosurgeon "—I want you to award her every consideration. From now on, Dr. DelMonico is to be your shadow, your sponge and your assistant." He emphasized the last word as his eyes locked with Ivan's. "Do I make myself clear?"

For his part, Ivan seemed completely unfazed. He merely nodded, his eyes and expression unreadable. "Perfectly."

His hand was on the doorknob. Bailey sprang to her feet. Her chair made a scraping noise as she moved it back and then quickly joined the neurosurgeon before he could leave the office.

Closing the door behind him, Ivan leaned over and whispered into her ear, "Just so you know, I'm going to be your worst nightmare."

Bailey DelMonico has finally
gotten her life on track, and is
passionate about her recent career
change. Nothing will stand in the way
of her becoming a doctor...that is,
until she's paired with the sharp-tongued
Dr. Ivan Munro.

Watch the sparks fly in

Doctor in the House

by *USA TODAY* Bestselling Author

Marie Ferrarella

Available September 2007

Intrigued? Read more at
TheNextNovel.com

HARLEQUIN®
Next™

HARLEQUIN®

Mediterranean NIGHTS™

Sail aboard the luxurious Alexandra's Dream and experience glamour, romance, mystery and revenge!

Coming in October 2007...

AN AFFAIR TO REMEMBER

by

Karen Kendall

When Captain Nikolas Pappas first fell in love with Helena Stamos, he was a penniless deckhand and she was the daughter of a shipping magnate. But he's never forgiven himself for the way he left her—and fifteen years later, he's determined to win her back.

Though the attraction is still there, Helena is hesitant to get involved. Nick left her once...what's to stop him from doing it again?

HM38964

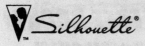

Romantic
SUSPENSE

**Sparked by Danger,
Fueled by Passion.**

When evidence is found that Mallory Dawes
intends to sell the personal financial information
of government employees to "the Russian,"
OMEGA engages undercover agent Cutter Smith.
Tailing her all the way to France, Cutter is
fighting a growing attraction to Mallory while at
the same time having to determine her connection
to "the Russian." Is Mallory really the mouse in
this game of cat and mouse?

Look for

Stranded with a Spy

by *USA TODAY* bestselling author

Merline Lovelace

October 2007.

Also available October wherever you buy books:

BULLETPROOF MARRIAGE *(Mission: Impassioned)*
by Karen Whiddon

A HERO'S REDEMPTION *(Haven)* by Suzanne McMinn

TOUCHED BY FIRE by Elizabeth Sinclair

REQUEST YOUR FREE BOOKS!

2 FREE NOVELS PLUS 2 FREE GIFTS!

SPECIAL EDITION®

Life, Love and Family!

YES! Please send me 2 FREE Silhouette Special Edition® novels and my 2 FREE gifts. After receiving them, if I don't wish to receive any more books, I can return the shipping statement marked "cancel." If I don't cancel, I will receive 6 brand-new novels every month and be billed just $4.24 per book in the U.S., or $4.99 per book in Canada, plus 25¢ shipping and handling per book and applicable taxes, if any*. That's a savings of at least 15% off the cover price! I understand that accepting the 2 free books and gifts places me under no obligation to buy anything. I can always return a shipment and cancel at any time. Even if I never buy another book from Silhouette, the two free books and gifts are mine to keep forever.   235 SDN EEYU   335 SDN EEY6

Name _____ (PLEASE PRINT) _____

Address _____ Apt. _____

City _____ State/Prov. _____ Zip/Postal Code _____

Signature (if under 18, a parent or guardian must sign) _____

Mail to the **Silhouette Reader Service™:**

IN U.S.A.: P.O. Box 1867, Buffalo, NY 14240-1867
IN CANADA: P.O. Box 609, Fort Erie, Ontario L2A 5X3

Not valid to current Silhouette Special Edition subscribers.

Want to try two free books from another line?
Call 1-800-873-8635 or visit www.morefreebooks.com.

* Terms and prices subject to change without notice. NY residents add applicable sales tax. Canadian residents will be charged applicable provincial taxes and GST. This offer is limited to one order per household. All orders subject to approval. Credit or debit balances in a customer's account(s) may be offset by any other outstanding balance owed by or to the customer. Please allow 4 to 6 weeks for delivery.

Your Privacy: Silhouette is committed to protecting your privacy. Our Privacy Policy is available online at www.eHarlequin.com or upon request from the Reader Service. From time to time we make our lists of customers available to reputable firms who may have a product or service of interest to you. If you would prefer we not share your name and address, please check here. ☐

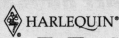

HARLEQUIN®

N^{TM}xt

GET $1.^{00} OFF

your purchase of any
Harlequin NEXT novel.

Receive $1.^{00} off

any Harlequin NEXT novel.

*Available wherever books are sold, including
most bookstores, supermarkets, drugstores
and discount stores.*

Coupon expires February 28, 2008.
Redeemable at participating retail outlets
in the U.S. only. Limit one coupon per customer.

5 65373 00076 2   (8100)0 11436

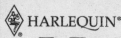

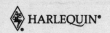

HARLEQUIN®

EVERLASTING LOVE™

Every great love has a story to tell™

An uplifting story of love and survival that spans generations.

Hayden MacNulty and Brian Conway both lived on Briar Hill Road their whole lives. As children they were destined to meet, but as a couple Hayden and Brian have much to overcome before romance ultimately flourishes.

Look for

The House on

Briar Hill Road

by award-winning author
Holly Jacobs

Available October wherever you buy books.